When Noah Lau joined the Vampire Hunters Association, seeking justice for his parents' deaths, he didn't anticipate ending up imprisoned in the house of the vampire he was supposed to kill—and he definitely didn't anticipate falling for that vampire's lover.

Six months later, Noah's life has gotten significantly more complicated. On top of being autistic in a world that doesn't try to understand him, he still hunts vampires for a living...while dating a vampire himself. Awkward.

When one of Jordan's vampire friends goes missing and Noah's new boss at the VHA becomes suspicious about some of his recent cases, what starts off as a routine paperwork check soon leads Noah to a sinister conspiracy. As he investigates, he and Jordan get sucked into a deadly web of intrigue that will test the limits of their relationship.

Human Enough

E.S. Yu

A NineStar Press Publication

Published by NineStar Press
P.O. Box 91792,
Albuquerque, New Mexico, 87199 USA.
www.ninestarpress.com

Human Enough

Printed in the USA
First Edition
October, 2019

Print ISBN: 978-1-951057-51-0

Also available in eBook, ISBN: 978-1-951057-50-3

Warning: This book contains sexual content, which may only be suitable for mature readers, ableism, graphic violence, allusions to past emotional abuse, abduction, and hate groups.

For the misfits.

Chapter One

As a vampire hunter, Noah was used to his plans going south in the worst possible ways. This op, however, was currently vying for one of the worst—by annoying him out of his goddamned mind.

On paper, it had sounded simple: a vampire had been responsible for some blood-drained corpses, probably a newly turned one based on how messy the crime scenes were, and Noah's squad had been assigned to take care of the problem. They were in the unusual situation of being down one member while waiting for their new squad leader to arrive, but the op should've been easily doable for a three-person team. According to their intel, the vampire always left his suburban house after sunset to feed. Except Noah was still sitting in a backyard tree five hours after sunset, watching the vampire's immobile heat signature through the second-floor window. His fingers were going numb in the cold autumn night, the colors from his infrared binoculars had practically been seared into his retinas, and he swore he was going to become part of the tree if he sat there for much longer.

He finally got Casey O'Donnell to cover for him—which Casey only agreed to after making some snide comments—while he texted Jordan.

Sorry, can't make it to the movie tonight. Hunt taking longer than expected.

And, after debating with himself as to whether a smiley face was too much, he finally added, ☺.

Jordan texted back quickly: *No worries. Be safe!!*

It was the third time he had to cancel plans with Jordan in two weeks, and it was making him cranky.

"Who were you texting?" Casey asked, again, from his perch on the opposite side of the tree.

"Someone," said Noah for the third time.

Casey was eyeing him in a way that made Noah uncomfortable. "That's the third time you've texted during a stakeout."

Jesus, he's keeping track? Noah put his phone away. "What, like you've never played Candy Crush on *your* phone during a stakeout?"

Casey raised an eyebrow. "I thought not breaking rules was your thing. Along with not being able to lie and stuff."

And there it is. Noah suppressed the urge to snort. Casey was half right...but he was also half wrong, as usual. While Noah generally preferred not to stir up trouble, he was perfectly capable of breaking rules and lying through his teeth if he thought it was for the "greater good," however he defined that. Which, in this case, meant passing on status updates so Jordan wouldn't be up all night worrying.

Noah raised the infrared binoculars to his eyes, turning the night back into neon colors, and scanned the second-floor bedroom again. Still no movement. He turned his comm back on. "Guys, the vamp might as well be asleep. We should move."

"No can do, Lau," said Ava Lopez through the comm. She was currently keeping watch at the front of the house. "He might use the human as a hostage if he smells us."

That was the problem, the reason why they'd been stuck out there for hours, waiting for the vampire to leave. Through his infrared binoculars, Noah could clearly see the human's heat signature in the same room as the vampire's dimmer one. There were any number of reasons why a human might be living with a vampire, but standard hunter protocol was to assume that a vampire valued human lives less than their own.

But what if that might not be true? an annoying voice asked in the back of Noah's mind.

His jaw tightened. He couldn't say that for sure, and human safety always had to come first, he reminded himself. Besides, the vampire had already crossed the line by killing people.

"Well, intel has clearly been faulty so far, so how much longer are we going to wait out here?" he groused. He *hated* faulty intel. At best, it scrambled their carefully created plans and forced them to improvise; at worst, it cost lives. Also, right now it was ruining the romantic movie night he'd planned.

There was silence at the other end as Ava thought. At least, Noah hoped she was thinking of a plan and not a rebuttal as to why they should sit and wait for another five hours.

"Okay," she finally said. "I'm thinking doorbell strategy. Anyone have any objections?"

"No, ma'am," Casey drawled.

The doorbell strategy was slightly risky for a three-person team. If they flushed the vampire out, they'd usually need someone to cover every side of the house. Noah couldn't think of any other feasible, safe alternative, though.

"All right," Ava said. "Move out."

Noah continued watching the window through the infrared binoculars. After a few minutes, the human heat signature left his view.

"The human's answering the door," Noah said over the comm.

"Copy that," said Casey. His boots scraped against bark as he climbed down from the tree. "What's the status on the vamp?"

"He hasn't moved," Noah observed.

The muted sounds of Ava's conversation with the house's human inhabitant sounded over the comm. Then, Ava said, "I'm going inside to flush him out. Be prepared."

Noah put his binoculars away and clambered down from the tree. "I'm at the south window," he said. Although the bedroom was on the second floor, vampires could survive jumping to the ground from that height with no problem.

"Got the west window covered," Casey added.

Noah readied his rifle. One minute passed. Then, another. Ava shouted at the vampire, her voice carrying through the comm a split second before gunshots followed.

Ava swore. "Missed him!"

Noah heard the sound of a window shattering—at the unguarded front of the house.

"He's escaping through the front!" he yelled. He ditched his rifle and drew his handgun from its holster as he bolted around the side of the house, toward the sound of breaking glass.

He raised his gun and shot as the vampire fell, but the vampire hit the ground, rolled to his feet, and immediately grabbed the human woman who'd been standing in the front yard, yanking her against him. She hadn't moved away from the house the way Ava had instructed her to. Noah's heart sank.

Oh, crap.

This was not the "easy, quick hunt and then go home" he'd been hoping for.

Casey came around the other side of the house behind the vampire. "Don't shoot," Noah said into the comm. "There's a hostage in front of him."

"Make one move, and the human goes!" the vampire shouted, keeping the woman in front of him as he turned to face Noah. The woman's eyes were wide with fear.

Noah hesitated, his finger perched on the trigger. His marksmanship was solid, but he still didn't want to risk shooting the woman. Ava was still in the house, judging by the way the vampire glanced through the open doorway, but her options were also limited.

"You don't have to do this," Noah said, and then nearly cringed when he realized he was reciting a line from basically every action movie ever.

The vampire bared his fangs next to the woman's neck. "I wouldn't have to if you *hunters* just left me alone!"

Noah's grip tightened on his gun. "You know what the punishment is for killing humans. You brought this on yourself."

The vampire's eyes narrowed. "You'd never under—"

He suddenly cried out, crumpling to his knees. The woman scrambled away from him, and Noah took the shot, nailing him in the chest. He crept closer, making sure to shoot the vampire in the heart several more times. The vampire didn't move after that.

"Death confirmed," Noah said into the comm. He glanced through the doorway into the house, to where Ava had knelt in the front hall to shoot the vampire in the knees. "Thanks."

Ava nodded at him as she got up. "No problem."

Casey came over to join them and whistled. "Shooting out his kneecaps? Impressive."

"Thanks, O'Donnell," said Ava.

"And nice job for finishing him off and keeping him distracted, Lau," said Casey. "But you know there's no point in reasoning with vampires, right?"

Noah didn't reply to that except to shrug. He went to grab the body bag from their van.

He and Casey stuffed the corpse into the bag—Casey moaned and groaned about being on cleanup duty, as always—while Ava made sure the woman was okay. She reported back to them that the woman was in shock, so after Noah and Casey lugged the bag and the rest of their gear back to the van, they dropped the woman off at a hospital. Noah hoped she would be okay.

"Whew," said Ava, once they'd dumped off the body for disposal and driven back to headquarters. "I don't know about you guys, but I could really use a drink. Anyone else up for a bar crawl?"

"Can't," Noah said immediately. "Sorry. It's pretty late, and I have to get back home. Maybe next time, though," he added, to be polite.

"What's the matter, Lau?" Ava teased. "Got a hot date?"

Before Noah could answer, Casey beat him to the punch. "It's his mysterious girlfriend he won't let anyone meet. What's her name again?"

"Jordan. And for the last time, she's shy and private and faints at the mention of blood," said Noah, the practiced lies rolling smoothly off his tongue. "Can't anyone keep their work life and private life separate anymore?"

"Aw, c'mon!" Casey nudged him. "Can't you at least show us a picture?"

Noah rolled his eyes. "I wouldn't want to give you any ideas, O'Donnell."

He said goodbye to his squad mates before they could ask him any more questions and drove back to his apartment. Damn, it was late. Wearily, he trudged up to his unit, unlocked his door, and slipped inside.

He made his way into the bathroom, stripped his clothes off, and stepped into the shower, sighing as the warm water hit his tired muscles. He closed his eyes, trying to let his mind drift away from work. A few minutes later, the shower curtain slid aside with a rustle and cool arms circled his waist.

"Long day at the office?" a soft, low voice murmured against his ear.

Noah smiled and leaned back. "Very long. Glad to be home at last."

"Me too."

Noah turned around to look at the hazel-eyed man with golden-brown hair and pale skin—a touch *too* pale—behind him.

"Hey, Jordan," he said, before leaning forward and kissing his boyfriend under the shower spray.

Noah always felt somewhat bad for lying about his "girlfriend" to his coworkers. It wasn't that he was afraid of people knowing he was dating a guy; he just didn't want anyone getting too interested in his dating life and finding out he was dating a vampire.

Chapter Two

SIX MONTHS EARLIER

"Rookie!" a gruff voice yelled, pulling Noah out of his thoughts. "Stop daydreaming and get your head in the game!"

Noah scowled. "I *do* have my head in the game. Sir."

"Then fucking *look* like it!" squad leader Eddie Jespersen bellowed from the opposite side of the van, his voice ringing in the confined space. "This is an *elite* hunt! You've gotta do more than sleepwalk and pop off a blood-drunk vamp flunkie this time!"

Noah resisted the urge to tell him that he'd been going over the details of the plan in his head, not "daydreaming." Elite hunts were rare, as vampires who were a hundred years or older typically got that way by being low-key and clever enough to avoid drawing the attention of the Vampire Hunters Association. Making it to an elite hunt had been his dream since he'd started working as a hunter a year ago; putting up with an obnoxious squad leader was, unfortunately, the price he had to pay.

Noah slouched back in his van seat with his rifle and closed his eyes, going over the plan again. Even though this wasn't his first vampire hunt by a long shot, he felt as jittery as a first-time hunter. He'd never faced a vampire that was older than a few years before, and this one was supposedly over one hundred years old.

Maybe it was the vampire that had killed his parents.

Probably not—even if no one knew how many vampires there were in the world, he doubted the statistics were in his favor.

Still, the possibility—as infinitesimal as it was—got adrenaline pumping through his veins before he reminded himself not to get cocky, because a cocky hunter was a dead hunter, as Rob always said. And if he died during a hunt, his sister would personally march into the afterlife and kill him again.

"Lau," Jespersen said again, his voice slightly quieter—which still put him at above average talking volume.

What now? Noah cracked his eyes open. "Sir?"

Jespersen was frowning at him. "Look," he said, "don't think I don't know you only got this gig because you're old friends with the director."

Noah's blood slowly began to boil in his veins at the mention of his connection with Rob. "Sir, I trained and *fought* for this position just like every other hunter." Sure, he was probably the youngest person on this team at twenty-five years old, but there were even younger hunter trainees.

Jespersen's expression didn't change. "I know you have autism."

Noah froze. He was hyper-aware of the six other hunters in the van, listening to the conversation, and helpless outrage at the blatant invasion of his privacy welled up in his throat, making him want to scream. He forced himself to breathe, slowly.

You might as well add that I'm pansexual while you're at it, he thought bitterly.

"I'm not going to coddle you like the director does, is all I'm saying," Jespersen went on. "If you screw this op up, it's your ass I'm going to nail to the wall. Clear?"

Not that Noah had ever asked for, nor expected, "coddling"; he'd only asked for *reasonable accommodations* when he'd had a desk job, like being exempted from taking phone calls and being allowed to wear earbuds while he worked, since he found it difficult to read and write up reports in a crowded office environment unless he could drown out the conversations with music or stimmy sounds. But that was the double bind with autism: people expected you to be either "too disabled" to do the job at all, or so "mildly disabled" that you should be held to the exact same standards as allistic—non-autistic—employees.

And the fact that Jespersen had not only publicly brought up Noah's diagnosis without his consent, but also accused him of being underqualified because he was neurodivergent and only getting the job through favoritism (*as if there weren't allistic VHA employees who were hired through personal connections*, Noah thought scornfully) made him want to punch somebody in the face. He swallowed the thought down, though. Going to jail for assaulting a fellow human was not one of his life goals, even if the human in question was an ableist dickwad.

Also, he didn't "have autism"; that made it sound like a contagious disease, like the flu. He was *autistic*. He doubted Jespersen was open to discussing semantics, though.

"Clear, sir," he gritted out.

Jespersen glanced out the window as the van slowed, parking off the road. "Okay team, we've arrived. Fan out!"

Noah gripped his rifle tightly as he got out of the van. He had a lot riding on this hunt, and he was determined not to screw it up.

He sucked at a lot of things—having a social life, keeping a romantic relationship—but he refused to suck at his job.

The vampire lived in Sudbury, a small town outside of Boston. The anonymous phone tip the VHA had received hadn't provided his address, but it *had* informed them which route the vampire would take when he returned from Boston late in the afternoon, and it had also told them what kind of car the vampire would drive, down to the license plate number. Said number had been registered to a "John Smith," which was the most obvious fake name Noah had ever heard. (No offense to the people who were *actually* named John Smith.)

The tip had given them the vampire's real name, though: Julius Saint Laurent.

Noah preferred to just call him "the vampire." His name didn't matter; he'd be dead soon enough.

The squad left the van and split up, half to cover each side of the road. The road they'd chosen was fairly rural, surrounded by trees—perfect for an ambush. Two hunters peeled away from the rest to take point, and Noah settled down on the south side of the road with Jespersen (unfortunately) and two other hunters behind the trees to wait for the vampire.

Breathe in, breathe out. Stay calm. If things went well, Noah might not have to lift a finger; elite vampires required combined mega-squads only in case something went wrong. Still, waiting was the most nerve-wracking part. It could easily dull the senses with boredom or suck him into a death spiral of anxiety.

Noah focused on replaying his most recent musical obsession in his head as though he were listening to it on loop on his phone. The afternoon dragged on into early evening, making the tree shadows stretch along the road like black, monstrous fingers as the sky burned and then deepened to indigo. Once in a while, the other hunters would murmur to one another, and he absently listened to their conversations. Always listening in, never being asked to join.

He started when the comm in his ear suddenly crackled to life. "Silver Ford Escape spotted." There was a pause, then the muffled sound of gunshots. "Tires hit."

"Copy that," Jespersen grunted. "Get ready."

Noah drew a deep breath, his finger resting on the trigger. Just in case something went wrong.

The Ford Escape roared into view, rubber squealing on asphalt as it careened wildly back and forth along the road with blown front tires. Just before it passed them, the car swerved off the road and crashed into a tree trunk—on the north side of the road.

The tension left Noah's muscles in a rush. So far, so good.

More gunshots peppered the air, along with the sound of breaking glass, as the north team shot into the car. Then, the noise stopped. Noah's ears rang in the sudden silence.

"Status?" Jespersen asked, his voice surprisingly quiet for once.

A moment of silence passed before one of the hunters answered. "The...the vamp's not in the car, sir."

"*Shit*," Jespersen hissed. "It escaped? You're sure?"

"There's no body."

Jespersen swore again. Noah's heartbeat faltered. If the vampire wasn't confirmed dead, then...where the hell was he?

"North team, search your side of the road, and we'll search ours. Use blood grenades. We are *not* going to let that motherfucker escape, got it?"

Noah bit down on his lower lip. That was assuming the vampire had been injured enough to slow him down; a healthy vampire could easily outrun a human search party.

But...what if the vampire isn't *trying to escape?* a fearful voice wondered in the back of his head. Splitting up the squad would be a bad idea if the hunters had now become the hunted. He internally shook his head at himself. *Jespersen may be an ableist dickwad, but he's squad leader for a reason.* Noah had his orders.

He put on his search goggles and flicked on infrared. The world turned into a palette of blues, punctuated by the bright reds and oranges of the other hunters. He took one of the blood-scent canisters at his waist that would hopefully lure the vampire while masking the scent of the hunters' blood and tossed his as the hisses of the others' canisters sounded from nearby. The stench of blood filled the air, so thick it made him gag.

He breathed through his mouth and scanned the blue landscape, searching for the vampire's heat signature as the cool evening wind scattered the blood scent. Nothing came up.

A loud crackle made him jump and swing his rifle around—before he recognized the human heat signature in his vision emerging from behind a tree.

"Whoa. Stand down, rookie, or you're gonna hurt someone," Jespersen growled.

Noah flushed with humiliation. "S-sorry, sir."

Jespersen sighed. "Nothing here so far," he muttered over the comm. "North?"

"Negati—"

The voice suddenly cut off with a scream. Noah froze. Shouts and gunshots echoed over the comm.

"It's here!"

"Get him!"

"He's on me! He's on—"

And then, it was silent.

Noah's blood had turned to ice. He realized his hands were shaking around his rifle.

"North?" Jespersen hissed. "*Anyone?*"

No response.

Jespersen swore. "Stick together," he commanded the rest of the hunters. "Wilson, my left. Thomas, my right. Lau, you bring up the rear."

Noah would rather have run. Run, and not stop running until he'd holed up in his apartment and locked the door with his deadbolt. He had to force himself to join the others, his breath stuttering in his lungs, searching the darkness with wide eyes to make sure the vampire wouldn't jump them.

He'd never witnessed hunters die during a hunt before.

He'd never *wanted* to witness hunters dying during a hunt before.

Noah shuffled backward, his back to his squad mates, as they crossed to the north side of the road. When he bumped into someone else's back, he realized they must've found the other hunters.

"Fuck," Jespersen breathed. "Thomas, any survivors?"

"Negative, sir," Thomas replied after a few minutes.

Noah's breath left him as though he'd been punched in the chest. *Oh God.* How had the vampire killed four hunters within the space of minutes? He'd thought they were prepared for this, but now he realized just how much he'd underestimated the elite vampire. He couldn't bear to turn around and look at the massacre—

"Get a hold of yourself, rookie," Jespersen growled. "Where is the fucking *vamp*?"

Noah gulped. Slowly, he turned around.

Just in time to see a new heat signature knock Jespersen to the ground and sink long fangs into his neck.

Terror ripped a yell from Noah's throat as he jammed his finger against the trigger of his rifle, firing. When his ammo ran out, though, Jespersen lay on the ground unmoving, but the vampire was nowhere to be seen.

"Where'd it go?" Wilson demanded, his voice unnaturally high.

"Lau, behind you!" Thomas cried, raising her gun at him.

Noah dove for the ground as Thomas fired. He rolled behind a tree, shoving his goggles away from his face as he reached with shaking fingers for another magazine. He swore as he almost dropped it before getting it into his rifle. Behind him, gunshots and curses filled the air.

"Oh sh—" There was a loud *crack.*

"Wil—" Thomas's voice abruptly cut out as the gunshots stopped.

It was silent.

Noah's breath came sharp and fast, his heart jackhammering in his chest as he huddled at the base of the tree. He wanted to whisper, *Hello? Is anybody there?* over the comm, but he was terrified the vampire would hear him and kill him too.

Though, if the vampire was close enough to hear him, he was damn well close enough to smell him, making Noah a dead man walking.

Noah clutched his rifle. *Run, or stay and hide?* If he ran, he risked discovery, but if he stayed, the vampire would smell him. And then kill him. Just like he'd killed—

No! Maybe they're still alive. Don't think about it.

He would make a run for it. There was no way he could possibly be expected to finish the mission by himself (*oh my God, stop thinking, stop thinking*). He took his two remaining blood-scent canisters and tossed them in random directions. Then, gripping his rifle tightly, he got to his feet and sprinted toward the direction of the VHA van.

The van was parked roughly twenty yards away. Grass rustled underfoot as the cold night air burned Noah's throat with each harsh, gasping breath. He saw the dark silhouette of the van emerge, and his heart leaped with hope. He was going to make it, he was going to—

Something grabbed him from behind and slammed him backward into the ground. He felt his rifle yanked away from his hands, just before a tall, pale man—no, *vampire*—loomed over him with ice-blue eyes and a terrifying smile.

"Oh, look. One more mouse. An Oriental mouse, too."

"Oriental"? I'm not a fucking rug. Noah's hand dove for his handgun, but he cried out as the vampire stomped on his hand, pinning it to the ground. The vampire plucked his handgun from its holster and tossed it away.

"P-please," Noah stammered, fear making tears slide down his face. "Please don't kill me."

"Humans. So boringly predictable." The vampire shook his head.

He yanked the comm from Noah's ear before sinking long fingers into Noah's shoulders, jabbing him. Before Noah could pry them off, the ground tilted sideways, wind roared in his face, and his stomach dropped as though he were on a roller coaster ride—and then he slammed into the ground again. But not dirt; this time, the ground was hard. Wood, he realized.

What the hell?

Fledgling vampires were marginally faster than humans. Older vampires, apparently, moved much, much faster than that.

He struggled to his knees, rubbing his shoulders furiously, and raised his head. He was in some sort of...house? But why? As he took in his surroundings, trying to process and wondering where the vampire had gone, he realized there was someone else in front of him.

Someone who was clearly not Julius Saint Laurent.

He was a young man who appeared a few years younger than Noah. Almost still a boy, in fact—maybe a college freshman? He wore a slightly oversized flannel shirt and faded jeans that made his oddly pale skin stand out, but even so, Noah could tell he was pretty. The kind of pretty that, if he'd been a few years older, Noah might've gotten himself drunk for in order to get the courage to ask him out. He had golden brown hair, wide hazel eyes framed by long eyelashes, and a small mouth with full lips.

Now was really not the time to think about potential hook-ups, though. Noah had no idea who this guy was, or why he was there, but he was probably in danger. Noah struggled to his feet.

"You have to get out of here," he rasped. "There's a vampire chasing me. He wiped out the rest of my squad."

The young man took a step back, his eyes widening.

"Please," Noah went on. "I don't know where the vampire went, but he could be right behind me—"

A laugh rang behind him, making him stop dead. "Oh, this is too precious."

Noah whirled around, his muscles tensing. His odds of killing the vampire by himself, without his weapons, were laughable, but he had to try. Whoever this young man was, Noah would *not* let him get sucked dry without putting up a fight.

Julius Saint Laurent smiled. "Look, darling," he drawled. "The human doesn't recognize what you are."

At first, Noah was baffled. *Why is this vampire calling me "darling"?* But when he cast a glance at the guy behind him, he realized the guy's gaze had dropped to the ground.

Noah's stomach dropped with it. *No...no way...*

He'd never seen a vampire who looked as young as this one did. It *couldn't* be...could it?

"Come now," Julius went on. "Don't play with your food."

The young man—*vampire*—flinched. His lips parted.

"I...I'm not thirsty," he said, his voice barely above a whisper.

Noah's blood ran cold. Against one vampire, he had a chance to escape, if a very slim one. Against *two* vampires?

Fuck my life.

Julius sighed. "Fine. I'll save him for when you *are* thirsty, then."

And then, before Noah could process what was happening, he was whisked away.

Noah's thoughts upon regaining consciousness were, in this order: *Fuck vampires. Fuck everything. Fuck—oh thank God, at least I get a toilet.*

He was in, weirdly, what appeared to be some kind of guest room, his ankle chained to the post of a bed frame. The chain was long, which struck him as bizarrely generous of his captors, as it allowed him to enter the attached bathroom and use the sink and toilet (but sadly, not the shower). He could almost reach the door, but he was pretty sure it was locked; besides, he couldn't exactly drag a bed frame out of the room behind him.

Noah tried everything he could think of to escape from the shackle or break the chain, but nothing worked. He spent several hours trying to pull the bed post he was attached to free of the rest of the frame but gave up when he was sure he'd managed to accomplish absolutely nothing. After exhausting himself, he curled up on the bed and managed to doze off, but he kept starting awake at the blood-spattered images and screams that haunted his sleep.

Maybe the VHA will send a rescue team. At least, he was sure they would send a team out to the van's location and hopefully save any of the other hunters who had survived. His own hopes for a rescue, however, were quelled by the fact that he didn't even know where he was, relative to the rest of Sudbury. He knew he'd ended up in a large, old-fashioned house, but he had no way of contacting anyone at the VHA to pinpoint his location, and it wasn't like the VHA could canvas every square foot of the town in order to find him. Noah cursed himself for leaving his phone behind in his VHA locker before he realized that if he'd had it, Julius Saint Laurent probably would've broken it, anyway.

He tried very hard not to think about how soon he would end up as a snack for the vampires, but it was almost impossible *not* to think about it. His panicking mind filled the long hours by composing his own obituary and imagining how pissed-off and heartbroken his sister would be to hear that he'd gone the same way as their parents.

That was the thought that upset him most.

The sound of a door opening wrenched him from his morbid thoughts, and he instinctively backed up against the headboard, heart thundering in his chest.

It was the younger vampire who stood in the doorway. Again, his apparent age took Noah aback; it made him look deceptively unthreatening. Based on the way Saint Laurent had called him "darling," Noah wondered if they were lovers. At first, Noah thought he'd come to drain his blood, but a second later he noticed the vampire was holding a tray in his hands. Noah blinked. It had food and a glass of water on it. The vampire carefully closed the door behind him, approached the bed with slow steps, and put the tray at the foot of it.

So the vampires were keeping Noah alive as some kind of...toy for their amusement? Fury and fear surged within Noah, making him glare at the vampire in hatred.

"Let me go," Noah snapped.

The vampire flinched.

"I'm sorry," the vampire murmured, his gaze downcast.

"Sorry?" The word was so absurd that it made Noah laugh bitterly. "*Sorry*? If you really were *sorry*, you'd let me go instead of keeping me for a snack."

The vampire flinched again. "I..." He hung his head. "I know. I'm sorry."

Noah stared at him, taking in his hunched shoulders. The vampire's voice had some sort of very faint accent. Southern, maybe? Noah carefully reached over for the bread roll on the tray and bit down on it. Stale, but it was fine.

"Yeah, right. I'm not going to believe that as long as you keep going along with your boyfriend's plan."

The vampire cringed at the word "boyfriend," but he didn't protest. "He doesn't listen to me," he said to the floor.

"What, does he have you under fucking *mind control* or something?" Noah spat. "You can't do *anything*?"

"He...he has the key," the vampire said, gesturing to Noah's shackle.

"And I guess you're too in love to steal it from him or anything, despite how *sorry* you are?"

The fact that the vampire kept reacting like a kicked puppy to his words only pissed him off further. But the vampire only dropped his gaze and didn't reply.

When Noah had finished eating, the vampire asked in a quiet voice, "What's your name?"

Noah eyed him with suspicion but, unable to figure out any sinister motive, grumpily answered. "Noah."

The vampire nodded. He collected the empty tray and made to leave the room.

"What's *your* name?" Noah called out, figuring an exchange was only fair.

The vampire paused by the door.

"Jordan," he finally answered, his voice whisper-soft. "Jordan Cross."

Then he slipped out of the room, closing the door behind him.

Chapter Three

Noah woke when he felt something next to him stir. As his grogginess slowly faded, he became aware of Jordan's limbs tangled comfortably around his. Jordan tended to be even more cuddly than usual after Noah came back from a hunt.

Jordan raised his head and blinked at Noah, smiling softly. "Morning."

"Morning." Noah brushed his lips against Jordan's. One of the weirder vampire superpowers: they never had bad morning breath. "What time s'it?"

"Ten fifty."

"What?" Noah sat up abruptly. "*Fuck.*" This was why he hated overnight ops with the passion of a solar flare.

"You came back late last night," Jordan pointed out gently.

"Yeah, and I missed *The Dark Knight* rerun, and now I've slept through half of the day." Having the broad strokes of his schedule disrupted felt like getting a massive mosquito bite in a place he wasn't able to scratch, and it drove him nuts.

"At least you're not late for work," Jordan said, giving him a calming squeeze. "And we'll still get to have most of the day together."

"Mm," Noah reluctantly conceded as he got out of bed and made his way to the kitchen in his pajamas, with Jordan following. He'd always thought one of the reasons he and Jordan got along so well was they were good at soothing each other's anxieties. Unlike his exes, Jordan was patient with Noah's quirks, while Noah didn't think less of Jordan when his demons reared their heads.

There was also the fact that they'd almost literally survived hell and high water with each other.

"In that case," Noah said as he threw some bread into the toaster, "I vote for rewatching *Batman v. Superman* instead of *The Dark Knight* this time."

Jordan's face lit up as he slid into one of the seats at the kitchen table. "Ohh, yes!"

Noah had been a big fan of *The Dark Knight* and its prequel for years, but *Batman v. Superman* had been a revelation with its gorgeous cinematography and soundtrack (seriously, the montage of the Waynes' deaths made him cry every time) and relatable, on-point portrayal of Batman as a man haunted by PTSD over the death of his parents. Almost *too* relatable for Noah.

"Made coffee for you when I got up a little while ago," Jordan said as Noah searched the cupboards. "It should still be warm."

Noah spied the full coffee pot on the counter and sighed with relief. "Thanks. You're a lifesaver," he said as he poured himself a mug. "Seriously, though, if I ever quit being a hunter, it'll be because of the overtime."

Jordan raised an eyebrow. "I'm pretty sure you're the only person who thinks working overtime is worse than actually, you know, risking life and limb to fight vampires every week."

Noah shrugged as he slathered peanut butter and jam on his pieces of toast and ate them separately. "Why, you don't think it's a crime when I lose time I could've been spending with you?"

He'd meant to sound suave and flirty; as usual, he missed the mark completely and sounded sullen and vaguely hostile instead. He winced, putting down his toast. "That…didn't come out right."

When he mustered the courage to look at Jordan's face, though, he realized Jordan was blushing.

"Do me a favor, Noah," Jordan said softly. "Don't ever change."

Noah looked down at the remainder of his toast, his chest feeling warm and bubbly. "Not a problem. You're stuck with my awkward flirting for life."

Jordan laughed, and Noah smiled.

After he finished eating, he got dressed for work. He paused at the front door to kiss Jordan goodbye. "Okay, I'm off to debrief Rob. See you after lunch?" Jordan usually worked part-time at the blood bank, but he'd switched shifts with one of his coworkers so he and Noah could enjoy the day together.

"I can meet you at Mango Red for lunch," Jordan said.

Noah blinked. As a vampire, Jordan didn't have a sense of taste (that extended beyond blood) anymore, and he really missed being able to taste food. Which made it awkward for them to eat out together, because Noah always felt kind of bad about eating right in front of him if he didn't need to.

"Are you sure? You don't have to…"

"I want to." Jordan smiled. "I can drink some bubble tea while you eat."

Noah's heart skipped a beat. "Okay. I'll see you there, then."

He tried to steal another quick kiss, but Jordan's fingers tangled in his hair, refusing to let him go. Noah pulled back reluctantly with a groan. "I'm supposed to get to work."

"You're no fun." Jordan's mischievous grin belied his words. Noah loved it when he looked like that—when he was happy, not weighed down by past regrets.

"Debriefing is serious business." He gave Jordan one last hug. "See you soon."

He was the last one of his squad to get to the office; Ava and Casey were lounging by Director Robert Bellamy's office, chatting, when he arrived. "Look who's late, for once," Casey said.

The warm, happy feelings Noah had had since talking to Jordan were beginning to fade. Casey was a skilled, reliable hunter, but he also often made Noah feel like he was on exhibit in a circus just because Casey couldn't seem to wrap his mind around the idea of an autistic who was verbal, understood sarcasm and innuendoes (mostly), wasn't obsessed with trains, and didn't rock or flap his hands. Noah would've resented him more if he'd been Noah's superior, or if he was more condescending; as it was, Noah just tried to ignore his comments. Or, on occasion, troll him—like when he acted surprised the first time he heard Noah swear, and Noah proceeded to utter a string of profanities that would've made a sailor proud.

"I'm not late. Our debriefing is scheduled for eleven thirty." He had cut it a bit close, though, thanks to oversleeping.

Casey smirked. "Had a busy night, did you?"

"Why," Ava interjected, "was yours not busy enough?"

Noah bit down on the urge to say, *I was busy sleeping, what were you doing?* "Anyway, let's just get the debriefing over with."

Ava knocked on the door. "Come in," the director called from inside the room.

Noah followed his squad mates in. Rob Bellamy, a tall white man in his early fifties with graying hair, looked up from where he was seated at his desk, giving them a broad smile.

"Ava, Casey, Noah. Good to see you all."

"Good to see you, sir," Noah said, echoing his squad mates.

Rob leaned back in his chair. "How did the hunt go last night?"

Ava kept her account concise and to the point. Rob nodded along.

"So, nothing out of the ordinary, then?"

"There was a slight deviation from the intel we received, sir," she said. "The vampire didn't leave the house to feed."

Casey snorted, rolling his eyes. "He probably just went out earlier. It wasn't *that* big of a deal."

"Did it impact the hunt?" Rob asked.

"Not really, but *some* people were unhappy that our stakeout ended up being much longer than expected." She glanced at Noah with a crooked smile, and Noah pretended not to hear her.

"Well, no harm, no foul, I suppose," Rob said. "Anything else you'd like to say?"

"No, sir," said Ava.

"Nothing to report," said Casey.

Noah stayed silent. Rob's easy dismissal of the inaccurate intel bothered him, but he wasn't sure he wanted to bring it up with everyone there.

"Great. Thanks for all your hard work, as always. Oh, and by the way," Rob added, "you have a new squad leader. She's transferring from the Atlanta branch and will be arriving in a few days."

"Finally," Casey grumbled. "I've been tired of only going after baby vamps."

"Speak for yourself, O'Donnell," Ava returned. "I'm not in a hurry to take on elite vampires."

They bickered as they filed out, but Noah hesitated before leaving Rob's office.

"Something on your mind, Noah?" Rob asked.

Noah tried not to go out of his way to talk to Rob one-on-one too often at work; having had one person accuse him of getting this job through nepotism was already one too many. Still, the faulty intel thing was bothering him.

"I think the intel problem is a major issue, sir. This isn't the first time it's happened recently, and there might be a future case in which it causes a hunter to get hurt—or worse." Noah would know; he'd barely escaped that kind of situation with his life before, and he was not eager to repeat the experience.

"I hear you. I've been meaning to check in with Investigations for a while, and I can make some inquiries, see if Anita's noticed any investigator getting sloppy. That should put your mind at ease."

Noah exhaled. "Thanks, sir."

"So...how are you doing lately?" Rob asked him with a smile.

Rob had been friends with Noah's parents, and he'd always been like an honorary uncle to Noah and his sister. When Noah applied to be a hunter, Rob became a mentor to him as well.

Noah shrugged. "I've been good."

"It's been a long while since we've gotten together for dinner. We should change that. I haven't talked to Elsie in ages."

"We've all been pretty busy," Noah pointed out. "And she's always off doing lawyerly stuff."

"Well, let me look at my calendar and figure out a time that might work for all three of us. I'm dying to catch up with both of you. Even though you and I work in the same department, I feel like I hardly see you anymore."

Noah chuckled, since it felt like that was the reaction expected from him.

"I'll contact both of you soon. But you're probably eager to get out and take some well-deserved relaxation time right now. Don't let me stop you," Rob said with another smile.

"Thanks," said Noah. "See you later, Rob."

Past experience had taught Noah that "soon" could mean anywhere from a few days to a few weeks to never. Not that Rob was insincere about getting together—Noah and his sister had had dinner with him once every few months—but allistics had a weird habit of making promises that they didn't mean literally, or easily forgot. Noah didn't really understand it, since if he made a promise, he felt duty bound to honor the terms he'd set out or else just not make the promise in the first place, but oh well.

He left Rob's office, eagerly looking forward to lunch.

Noah was a self-professed bubble tea addict, and Mango Red, his favorite bubble tea joint, was packed due to the lunchtime rush, as usual. The café gave off a cozy hipster vibe with its wooden décor, spotless white walls, and hanging lamps. Luckily, he spied Jordan sitting at a corner table with a cup of bubble tea—even if he couldn't taste the tea, he liked the texture of the chewy tapioca. Noah made his way over.

"Hey," he said, smiling.

"Hi." Jordan smiled back. "Sorry for ordering without you—I wanted to grab a table."

"No worries at all. I'll grab my food and be right back."

Noah ordered a Nutella-drizzled waffle, pork bun, and strawberry bubble tea and briefly recapped his talk with Rob to Jordan while he ate.

Jordan frowned over his bubble tea. "But faulty intel is a serious problem. I mean, what if it causes hunters to get injured on the job...or worse?"

Noah knew Jordan worried about the dangerousness of his job, but in typical Jordan fashion, he'd never tried to dissuade Noah from it.

"I know. Rob said he'd look into it, so let's hope he figures out what the problem is." Noah ate another bite of his Nutella waffle and grunted. "Maybe it's Anita in Investigations."

"Well, someone had better get on it," Jordan muttered. "Or else next time you get an overnight op, I'm not going to be able to sleep."

"Hey." Noah slid his hand across the table and gave Jordan's a quick squeeze. "I'll be fine, okay? You know I'm careful."

"I know you are." Jordan gazed back at him steadily. "That doesn't mean you'll never run into a vampire that outclasses you. Again."

A shiver ran down Noah's spine at the memory of Julius Saint Laurent.

"I'm sure they'll sort it out," he said with determined confidence.

"Okay," said Jordan, but he didn't sound totally convinced.

Noah didn't want to ruin his most-of-the-day off, so he searched for another topic. "How was your meeting yesterday?"

Unfortunately, the topic didn't seem to cheer Jordan up, even though he usually enjoyed his Vampire Survivors of Violence meetings. "It was good," he said without smiling.

Noah ate the last bite of his waffle. "But?" he said tentatively.

Jordan took another sip of tea before replying. "Remember Amy?"

"Yeah?"

"She hasn't shown up in a while, and that's kind of strange."

"Huh." Amy was one of the regulars at the meetings Jordan attended. "You don't think something's happened to her, do you?"

"I don't know. The others were also kind of worried. I just hope she's okay," Jordan murmured.

"Well," said Noah, "I'm not sure how much help I can be, but on the off-chance I hear something through the VHA, I'll let you know."

Of course, if he did hear something through the VHA, that probably meant Amy had been caught snacking on a human and was therefore targeted for elimination, so it wouldn't exactly be good news. "Thanks," Jordan said all the same, giving him a small smile. "I appreciate that."

Both of them were solid introverts, but they deviated from their usual habit of relaxing at home and made their way downtown, chatting about TV shows and whatever caught their eye along the way. Winter was slowly spreading through Boston, so this was one of their last opportunities to enjoy walking around outside before the bitter cold descended. They wandered past the bustling Quincy Market down to the harbor. Jordan, having grown up inland, drank in the sight of the deep blue horizon and passing sailboats while Noah watched him fondly, the salt-soaked breeze ruffling his hair.

"I'm still waiting for the day we can go to Cape Cod," Jordan said, throwing Noah a look.

Noah got a kick out of the fact that Jordan was so fascinated by the ocean he actually wanted to vacation at the beach. Even though when vampires were exposed to too much sun, their skin tended to flake off. When Noah had brought that up before, Jordan merely waved his hand, saying that was the reason why sunscreen had been invented.

"We'll go next summer," Noah said, grinning at him.

Jordan smiled back. "Promise?"

"Promise."

Of course, just as Noah thought that the day was perfect, he jinxed the whole thing.

As they made their way across a park, he caught sight of a bunch of people gathered together, holding signs as though they were protesting something. He was too far away to see what the signs said, though. "What do you think they're doing over there?"

Jordan's brow wrinkled. "Not sure."

Curiosity got the better of Noah, and he began walking in the direction of the group. He saw the word "vampire" on their signs and blinked. Vampires had been public knowledge for nearly thirty years. Noah was too young to remember the years when proof of vampires started to accumulate in the public eye, generating more and more fear and controversy, until the VHA—then still called the Van Helsing Agency—finally revealed to the world that, yes, vampires existed, and there were hunters to protect humanity from the vampire scourge. (They also busted some popular myths about vampires, such as that they burst into flames under the sun or couldn't enter a house without being invited.) Recently, some vampire rights groups had emerged to oppose the VHA, though they mostly operated on the internet instead of rallying in broad daylight.

But when he took a closer look at the protesters' signs, he stopped, swearing under his breath. "Oh, *fuck* no."

"Noah—"

"Hey! Hey, *you!*" Noah marched over to the protesters, almost knocking down another park visitor on his way. He jabbed a finger at their signs. "What the hell do you have against vaccinations?"

Thanks to science, everyone knew that the change from human to vampire was caused by a unique virus, one that caused the human body to cannibalize its own red blood cells. After many years of research, a Nobel-prize-winning vaccine had been developed to immunize people from becoming vampires. Which was useful considering that it wasn't too difficult to turn someone into a vampire. Although the virus had a low chance of surviving in a new host body individually, a large enough transfusion of vampire blood was guaranteed to trigger the change. It was even possible to forcibly turn a human into a vampire, as vampires began the process by draining humans of part of their blood, leaving them delirious enough that they couldn't put up much resistance.

One of the protesters, a guy who appeared Noah's age, curled his lip as he turned to Noah. "They're unsafe. It's all a conspiracy by Big Pharma to capitalize on anti-vampire hatred by exposing people to toxins."

"That's bullshit," Noah seethed. "There has been *no* scientific proof of toxins in the vampirism vaccines—"

"Oh, yeah? What about autism rates among children who take the vampirism vaccines?"

And this, *this* was why Noah absolutely hated anti-vampire-vaxxers. They may have been only a splinter group of vampire rights activists—the biggest group, the Hemovore Rights Coalition, was careful to skirt the issue of the vaccinations—but they still did a lot of damage. They were shameless in piggybacking off the general anti-vaccine hysteria spread by people who believed it was literally better to have their children die of preventable diseases than have them be autistic. In other words, anti-vaxxers didn't want people like him to exist.

"There is no. Fucking. Connection. Between vaccines and autism!" Noah shouted. "And stop talking as though being autistic is the worst thing that someone could be!"

"Noah." Jordan tugged at his arm, murmuring, "You probably shouldn't be seen here."

Noah tried to calm down. That was true—if anyone managed to figure out a member of the VHA was facing off with the protesters, the pro-vampire media would be all over it. "Fine," Noah said, gritting his teeth as he stepped back.

The activist turned to Jordan. "Brother, why do you throw in your lot with those who call you an abomination?"

Not all vampire rights activists were vampires, but Noah was hardly surprised to realize this one was, given the way he'd addressed Jordan—it was impossible for humans to distinguish between vampires and humans at a glance, but vampires could do so by smell. Jordan went very, very still. "Don't drag me into this," he said, his voice going uncharacteristically cold.

"The humans have brainwashed you into hating your own—"

"No one has *brainwashed* me into doing anything," Jordan snapped even as he started pulling Noah away. He added over his shoulder, "And stop telling people not to vaccinate!"

Both of their moods were off as they took the T back to Noah's apartment, and Noah kept trying to come up with more and more varied ways to curse the vampire anti-vaxxers out. When his fury finally began to simmer down, though, he began shooting glances at Jordan, who kept his eyes fixed out the window. Jordan wasn't easily angered, but Noah was pretty sure he'd been deeply insulted by the "brainwashing" remark given his history.

When they got back to the apartment, Noah nudged Jordan's shoulder. "The guy's an asshole. He doesn't know anything about what you went through."

"I know."

Noah chewed his lower lip. "Are you okay?"

"I will be." Jordan glanced at him. "I'm more upset by what he said to you. I'm so sorry."

Noah blinked, surprised. "Why are you sorry? It's not like it was your fault."

"What he said was awful and it hurt you, didn't it?"

Noah glanced away, shrugging. "It's not anything I haven't heard before."

In a sad way, he'd almost become used to defending himself while other people looked on skeptically or told him to *stop taking things so seriously.*

Jordan took a step closer to him and, after a second, held his arms out. "Hug?"

Noah's breath snagged in his throat. He moved into Jordan's arms, sighing as Jordan gently squeezed him.

"I think you're great just the way you are," Jordan murmured. "You know that, right?"

A sudden lump rose in Noah's throat, and he blinked hard at the heavy wetness in his eyes. "Yeah, I—I know," he whispered.

But the words never failed to take his breath away every time.

When he pulled back, Jordan let him go. "So...movie?" Jordan asked.

Noah smiled. "*Yes*." There was still hope for salvaging the day yet.

Chapter Four

SIX MONTHS EARLIER

It was strange, how easily terror could turn into boredom.

At first, Noah waited in a constant state of anxiety for something bad to happen to him. However, for reasons he couldn't figure out, Jordan Cross didn't seem inclined to drink his blood in a hurry, and when nothing happened for four days, Noah began to wonder if Julius Saint Laurent had somehow forgotten about him. Fear became jadedness, which became mind-numbing, soul-crushing boredom. Neither Julius nor Jordan had drained him yet, no VHA rescue party had shown up, Noah could see no way to escape from his shackle, and in the meantime, he had nothing to do.

After their first conversation, he didn't speak to Jordan, and Jordan didn't speak to him either, even though he always waited in the room with Noah until he finished eating. Eventually, though, Noah got tired of the silence. He needed *someone* to talk to, even if that someone was a vampire.

"How long are you going to keep me here?" he asked.

Jordan flinched. "I...I don't know," he whispered.

Clearly, he wasn't the one who made the decisions around here. His face was so downcast that it pissed Noah off. *He* wasn't the one who was chained up in a room, waiting to be turned into vampire food.

"What do the two of you do all day?" Noah asked. Irritation was making him abrasive. "Sleep in a coffin? With each other?"

Jordan winced.

"He...he goes out," he answered in a soft voice. His voice was always soft; Noah wondered if he ever raised it. "I just...read. And watch TV sometimes."

"Read," Noah echoed. Normally, this would've been his favorite topic...except for the fact that he was discussing it with a vampire who could drain his blood at any moment. "What kinds of books?" he asked with reluctant curiosity.

"Oh...anything that's around. Even appliance manuals." Jordan's mouth twitched a little, as though he were trying to smile, though Noah couldn't tell if he was serious or joking. The attempted smile was gone before Jordan could even complete it, though, as he returned his gaze to the floor. "Julius has a lot of old books, and not a lot of new ones. I like Isaac Asimov and Harry Potter, I guess."

Holy crap. Noah liked sci-fi, but even he hadn't gotten around to reading Asimov yet—it had slipped way down on his to-do list in between graduating from college, getting a job at the VHA, switching to being a hunter, and trying to do better at romantic stuff. And Harry Potter, a.k.a. Noah's entire childhood...he silently groaned. Why did he have to be talking to a *vampire* who liked *Harry Potter*?

Jordan bit his lower lip as he looked at Noah through his lashes. "Do...do you like to read?" he asked, hesitantly.

Against his better judgment, Noah answered, "Yeah. Sci-fi and fantasy books, mostly. And superhero comics."

"Superheroes," Jordan echoed. "Like Batman?"

Noah's throat almost sealed shut. "Yeah. Exactly like Batman."

"I haven't read many comics, but I saw the recent movie. I think it was called *Batman Begins*? It was really good."

Oh, shit. Noah's kryptonite. "Yeah, it was great. I think I've watched it like, twelve times. Have you seen the sequel?" When Jordan shook his head, Noah went on, "Oh man, you have to watch it. *The Dark Knight*—it's a classic. It's just too bad the last movie in the trilogy, *The Dark Knight Rises*, was pretty meh. Most of the time, I pretend that movie never happened. Actually, they rebooted Batman again with *Batman v. Superman: Dawn of Justice*, which just came out a few months ago. A lot of people were divided on the film, which kind of sucks to me because I *loved* it. I didn't think anyone could top Christian Bale's Batman, but Ben Affleck totally—"

Wait. What the hell am I doing?

He was talking to a vampire—whom he was supposed to kill if he ever escaped from this place alive, and who'd probably kill him before he ever got to that point. He wasn't talking to a *friend.*

"What?" Jordan asked, wide-eyed.

Noah looked away. "Nothing. Forget it."

"Oh." Jordan's voice was quiet. "Okay."

He sounded...resigned? Disappointed? Noah inwardly shook his head at himself. No, he was probably overreaching.

The next time Jordan visited—with a brunch of bread and cold pasta—Noah asked, "How come you don't go out? With your boyfriend?"

Jordan flinched again. Noah wondered if he was wrong about the whole "lovers" thing...but Jordan hadn't corrected him so far. Then he wondered if Jordan just came from a more conservative time period, which brought Noah back to the question: Exactly how old was Jordan, anyway?

Jordan put the food down in front of Noah and didn't answer right away. *Trouble in undead bloodsucking paradise?* Noah wondered.

"I guess I'm not a fun person to be around," he finally said as he leaned back against the wall.

Noah frowned. Now he was really curious, except asking felt like it would be too personal. "You must be really...uh, bored, if you're coming to *me* for conversation."

Jordan blinked at him. "Why? You're...um, you seem like a nice person."

"How do you know?" Noah asked.

Jordan stared. Too late, Noah realized he'd just asked one of those questions that made perfect logical sense in his head—*We barely know each other, so how do you know I'm nice?*—but sounded way too blunt when he said it out loud.

"Um..." Jordan tilted his head. "I don't know, you just...do?"

Thinking he was probably better off just nodding and moving away from this clearly failed conversation entirely, Noah picked up the bread from the tray and began to eat. Awkward conversations were the story of his life, though he was used to other people walking away once they realized his conversational skills were somewhere south of normal. Why Jordan kept sticking around...well, "bored" was the only explanation Noah could come up with.

Jordan shifted against the wall. "So...did you become a hunter because you hate vampires?" he asked, his voice soft.

He must be very, very *bored*, Noah thought. Or maybe speaking to a vampire hunter was a masochistic novelty for him.

"Um...sort of, but not really?" Noah swallowed the last piece of bread and gazed directly at Jordan. "My parents were killed by a vampire when I was a kid."

He'd said the words often enough that his voice came out flat, but the memories still brought a lump to his throat. He'd been eight years old then, and his parents told him and his sister that they would be home late, since they were helping a friend move. Back then, Noah had been excited because he and Elsie could stay up late playing Nintendo 64 on a weekday. He never expected police officers would visit them late at night to explain that their parents had been attacked on their way back and would never come home.

Jordan blanched. "Oh," he breathed, looking down. "I'm so sorry."

His reaction felt satisfying to Noah...but also strangely unsatisfying at the same time. Noah cleared his throat. "Yeah, well...so I applied for a job at the VHA after I graduated from college, but not as a hunter—as an investigator instead."

"Investigator?"

"Yeah. Investigators are the ones who verify that a vampire attack really happened and do all the legwork to figure out which attacks can be attributed to a single vampire and who that vampire is." Thanks to modern awareness, there were plenty of obfuscating cases of people who committed murders but tried to make them look like vampire attacks, or savvy vampires who tried to disguise their attacks as regular human murders. And trying to figure out whether a series of vampire attacks was due to one vampire or several was no mean feat. The scale of vampire attacks in the modern day, and the ability to identify more victims thanks to technology, was why investigation work had to be separated out from the pure hunting part.

"So...you didn't apply to be a hunter, then?" Jordan asked.

"No. My sister was very much against it, and I didn't really crave that kind of high-adrenaline life." Noah knew what people expected—*Oh, you hate vampires because they killed your parents? That* must've *been why you decided to become a hunter.* At no point did most people realize that he was, or had been, perfectly happy assisting the VHA from a less trigger-happy angle.

"What happened after that?"

Noah swallowed. "I was...almost fired."

"Why?" Jordan asked.

"I had a sucky boss," said Noah, shortly, "who kept harping on me for my 'shitty bedside manner.' She seemed to think I was terrible at interviewing witnesses, but I think she just had it out for me."

Noah didn't think he'd been *that* bad with the witnesses; he often copied what his coworkers said, which seemed to work. He was ninety-nine percent sure his boss, Anita Price, didn't like him for being autistic ever since Noah tried explaining why he couldn't really handle phone calls at work.

"The director of the hunter operations was an old family friend," Noah went on, "and he suggested transferring over to his wing instead. So, that's how I ended up here." Not that being a hunter was easy, but at least he didn't have to be evaluated based on his social interactions with other people, as long as he could get along with his squad.

Jordan had clasped his hands in front of him, his brow furrowed. "I'm really sorry about your previous job," he said in a soft voice.

Noah shrugged, unsure of what to do with Jordan's sympathy. "Life sucks sometimes."

"Yeah," Jordan murmured. "That's true."

Noah glanced at him. There it was again—that hint that Jordan was unhappy for some reason. "Well, now you know my story. What's yours?"

"Mine?" Jordan echoed.

"Yeah."

Jordan looked away. "Not much to tell," he said, almost mumbling. "I became a vampire. I've been a vampire for...a long time."

Okay, then. So Jordan was being evasive. That didn't quite seem fair to Noah, but oh well. "So...you're not really a teenager, are you?" Noah asked.

Jordan barked out a laugh, startling him. "No. Not even close."

Frankly, even if Noah wanted eternal life and youth, he wouldn't have wanted to look like a college student forever. "How old are you?"

Jordan seemed to hesitate. When he finally spoke, the words were barely audible. "Uh...ninety-five years old."

Holy shit. Ninety-five? It boggled Noah's mind that Jordan was old enough to be his freaking *grandfather* and yet still looked like a teenager. He tried to do the mental math. "That means you were born in..."

"1921," Jordan finished for him, eyes downcast. "Yeah."

Instead of bragging, Jordan seemed vaguely uncomfortable with the subject. Not that Noah was the greatest at reading people—to put it very, very mildly—but he didn't know how else to interpret Jordan's hesitance. Wasn't the whole draw of being a vampire the immortality thing, though? It was why the government had had to institute mandatory anti-vampire vaccinations—because of the not-insignificant number of people who thought that having to subsist off blood was worth effectively living forever.

"Um...that's cool," said Noah, not knowing how to deal with the suddenly awkward atmosphere.

Jordan grimaced. *Crap.* Wrong thing to say, apparently.

Searching for something else to say, Noah blurted out, "I haven't talked to anyone as old as you." As soon as the words were out of his mouth, he wanted to kick himself. What kind of thing to say was *that*?

Jordan stared at him for a moment. Then, without warning, he burst into laughter. It was strange-sounding laughter, with a slightly hysterical edge. Noah couldn't tell whether it was a good sign or whether Jordan was having a breakdown.

"Sorry?" Noah tried, his confusion turning the word into a question.

Jordan dragged the sleeve of his shirt across his face. "No, it's just...I don't think anyone's ever referred to me as 'old' before."

"Isn't ninety-five old? Even for a vampire?" Noah said before he could stop and think about whether Jordan might be offended at being called "old." *Ugh, I have to stop talking.*

"Yeah. It's just..." Jordan's expression sobered as he gestured at himself. "You know. Judging books by their covers."

"Right. I guess that kind of sucks." Noah hadn't really stopped to consider it before—outside of the popular jokes about teenaged vampires who could stay in high school forever—but then again, he knew what it felt like to be judged at a glance.

"Yeah," said Jordan, softly.

After he left, Noah found himself wondering about what Jordan's real, genuinely happy laughter sounded like, and he shook his head at himself.

Since when had he gone from hating Jordan to wanting to make him laugh?

Chapter Five

A low chuckle from behind him made Noah turn around. "Huh?"

"Your hair's sticking up all over the place." Jordan cupped a hand in the kitchen sink, collecting some tap water from the faucet, and gently pawed at Noah's hair, trying to smooth down the errant black tufts.

"Oh...thanks," Noah said, embarrassed. He was more than a little scatterbrained this morning. "It would've been bad to go to work like that."

"To show up to a hunt with a bad hair day?"

"We're meeting the new squad leader today," Noah explained.

"Ah." Jordan gave him a reassuring smile. "I hope she's nice."

Noah sighed. "Hope so." Or he would settle for a squad leader who was competent and more or less ignored him.

"So, she's leading you guys for the hunt?"

"Yep." Noah smoothed down his hair again, combing it with his fingers. "Guess we'll see her in action with our team soon enough."

After he'd dressed, Jordan took his face in his hands and gave him a slow, gentle kiss. "Be careful, okay?" he said softly.

"I will. Don't worry," Noah promised.

He got to the VHA, making a detour to get a cup of coffee from the break room first, to find Ava and Casey already waiting restlessly in the briefing room.

"Look alive, guys," Casey said as they waited in the conference room. "Wouldn't want to make a bad impression on our new squad leader."

For once, Casey was saying something sensible. Noah sipped his coffee, trying to wake himself up, though he wondered if the caffeine was making his jittery nerves worse. He was pessimistic by nature, and he kept wondering what he'd do if the new squad leader turned out to be another Jespersen.

"Who are you, and what have you done with Casey O'Donnell?" Ava drawled.

"Hey, I care about our squad's reputation, you know."

The conference room door swung open, and everyone shut up. Rob entered the room along with a tall, elegant black woman whom Noah guessed to be in her thirties.

"Delta Hunter Squad, I'd like you to meet your new squad leader, just transferred from the Atlanta branch—Ariel Cross."

A shiver of surprise went down Noah's spine at the name *Cross*. But...even if it wasn't *that* common of a last name, there still had to be enough people named Cross that she didn't necessarily have a connection with Jordan...right?

"Ariel is from the Cross family of vampire hunters in the South," Rob went on. "She's had a stellar record as a hunter for the Atlanta branch, and I couldn't be more thrilled to welcome her to Boston."

Noah had never heard of the Cross family of vampire hunters before. Granted, he didn't really keep track of these kinds of things. He only knew of the Van Helsing family because, well, *everyone* knew of the Van Helsing family. They'd only founded the VHA and were famous enough to have been mentioned in Bram Stoker's seminal novel (though scholars disagreed on whether it was a portrait of real events, with some exaggerations, or more like a collection of popular myths).

Also, if there *had* been some connection to Jordan, he was pretty sure Jordan would've mentioned it at some point already. "You're a vampire hunter? Hey, I have hunters in my family, too!" seemed like a pretty good conversation-starter to him.

"I'm excited to be here," Ariel said with a smile. "Although I'm a little less excited about dealing with the New England winters."

Noah joined the others in laughing at her joke.

"It's worth braving the cold to get a chance to work with the famous Rob Bellamy, though," she added, turning her smile his way.

Rob waved dismissively. "Oh, I'm not sure my reputation is worth more than the snow we get up here."

More laughter all around.

"It's a pleasure to meet you all," she said. "I've heard great things about this squad, and I look forward to serving as your squad leader."

They went around for introductions. Ariel Cross seemed nice enough, so Noah decided to remain cautiously optimistic; then again, he'd had plenty of experiences with people who had seemed nice when he first met them, only to turn on him later for reasons unknown.

"Well, then." Rob clapped his hands together. "I'll leave you guys to your briefing, then. Good luck, Delta Squad. Not that you'll need it, I'm sure." He winked at them before leaving.

Ariel took a remote from the conference table and turned on the screen behind her, displaying some pictures of a middle-aged white man.

"Our target today is Charlie Bunn. Fledgling vampire, turned about one month ago. At least three deaths have been attributed to him." She pressed a button, replacing the photos with a picture of a colonial house. "He's located in Watertown and works at night. He lives alone, so we'll get him in his house. Should be a straightforward, in-and-out elimination. Any questions?"

Noah shook his head. So did his squad mates.

"Okay." She nodded. "Get prepped and meet in the loading area."

They drove out to Watertown in one of the VHA's unmarked vans and parked on a street lined with old colonial houses.

"So," said Casey, cheerfully, once the van had come to a stop, "who wants front-door duty? Lau?"

"You could always go yourself," Ava cut in, "instead of volunteering other people."

Casey rolled his eyes. "Just looking for a partner to greet the vamp with. Of *course* I'm going."

"O'Donnell and I will take point, then," said Ariel, calmly, "and Lopez and Lau, you two will back us up."

Noah did his best to swallow his irritation at Casey's antics down for the sake of the mission. They approached the front door, and Casey bounded up the front steps to ring the doorbell.

Noah took a long, slow breath, keeping his hands ready on his gun. A minute passed. Two.

The door opened, and—

Wait, Noah thought. *The hell? That's not the vampire...*

The woman standing in the doorway seemed understandably freaked out at the sight of four people with guns on her porch. "What is this?" she said, her voice shrill. "What—"

"Sorry to bother you, ma'am," Casey said smoothly. "Do you live here?"

"Y-yes, with my brother..."

"We're from the VHA and we're looking for Charlie Bunn. Do you know where he is?"

The loud slam of a back door made Noah start. He swore and made a dash for the backyard.

"Lives alone," my ass.

He vaulted over the fence, and when he landed, he flicked down his infrared visor. A person-shaped blob of orange flickered in his vision, darting behind a house. He followed, aiming at the vampire's back, and squeezed the trigger.

The vampire staggered as the bullet hit him in the shoulder. He spun around, fangs flashing in his mouth. "Wai—"

Another gunshot split the air, and the vampire fell. As Noah stared, Ariel appeared from behind the next house over and shot the vampire again in the heart.

Casey followed behind her, letting out a whistle. "Nice one, boss."

"Thank you."

"No offense to your 'rush 'em' strategy," said Casey, turning to Noah with a cheerful grin.

"Whatever." Noah switched the safety back on for his rifle and slung it over his back. "You know," he said through his teeth, "I'm *really* tired of Investigations screwing up and giving us half-baked intel. We nearly lost him today because they said he lived—"

"Hold on," Ariel interrupted. "Has this happened before? Problems with intel?"

"Yeah," Noah seethed. "More often than just an occasional slip-up."

"How—"

A sudden cry interrupted them. "Murderers!"

The woman from before rushed over to the vampire's body, uttering a sob.

"Ma'am," Casey said, "Charlie Bunn was a vampire who was confirmed to have killed several humans—"

"*No.*" She shook her head. "He didn't kill anyone."

"Respectfully, ma'am, you don't know that," said Casey, his tone sharpening a little.

"*You're* the ones who don't know anything," she shot back. Her eyes were bright with tears, and Noah had to look away from her face. "You—you people from the VHA are just targeting any vampire you find, aren't you? You should be ashamed of yourselves."

"Ma'am—"

"Just leave me alone!" She curled protectively over the vampire's body. "Leave me alone."

Lost, Noah looked to Ariel. She frowned but tilted her head toward their van.

"Let's go." In a lower voice, she added, "We'll send someone for the body later."

On the way back, Casey muttered, "Back in the old days, people were grateful when hunters took down vampires. Now they get mad. What's the world coming to?"

Noah tried to tell himself that she was just upset, as one of the rare humans who'd accepted a family member-turned-vampire, but a sense of unease hung over him all day long.

"Hey. Hello? Earth to Lau?"

Noah blinked, rousing himself from his daze. "What?"

Casey was leaning against the wall of his cubicle. "You heading out soon?"

"Um...not yet. I'm going through some paperwork." Though Noah hadn't been all that productive that afternoon, having been distracted by the events of the morning

"Look at you, being such a hard worker," Casey said, smiling.

Noah had no idea if that was supposed to be teasing or not. Damn allistics and their inconsistent vocal inflections.

"Uh...thanks? Do you need something?" Noah asked when Casey didn't make a move to leave.

Casey shrugged. "Just wanted to chat. Seeing as we're squad mates and all, but I feel like I barely know you outside of work."

Noah stared at him. Where was *this* coming from? They'd already been working with each other for over four months. "What do you want to know?" he asked, confused.

"Who you hang out with in your free time, for starters. Are all of your friends autistic?"

"Yes," Noah deadpanned. "We're a hive mind."

Casey's blank look told him that his sarcasm had missed its target.

"Why do you want to know?" Noah asked, still weirded out by Casey's sudden interest.

"Just asking for a friend—a cousin of mine, actually, whose kid has autism, and who was wondering how people with autism make friends."

Noah rolled his eyes so hard they were in danger of getting permanently stuck in the back of his head. "The same way everyone else does, I guess."

"Really?" Casey asked. "It's not different because of the autism thing?"

"Was there anything else you needed, O'Donnell?" Noah asked, making a show of shuffling through his stack of folders.

"I was just going to say, you owe us a bar crawl, remember? I was thinking maybe tonight. You should invite your friends along—the more, the merrier." Casey waggled his eyebrows. "You can even bring your mysterious girlfriend."

No, thanks. Again, the last thing Noah wanted was for his coworkers to take an interest in exactly who he was dating. Besides, he did not do well with last-minute plans. He rubbed his forehead. "I've...got plans for tonight. Maybe next time, though."

"Plans with the girlfriend?" said Casey, grinning.

"*Plans,*" Noah said, resisting the urge to roll his eyes again. "Plans that include getting through this stack of reports."

"Sure, sure, Mr. Hard Worker." Casey flicked his fingers over his shoulder in a dismissive wave. "You ever want social tips, come over any time."

Noah glared at his computer screen after Casey left. He knew he'd been curt with him, but he'd been annoyed. And yet Casey's words had still slipped under his skin like unexpected barbs.

He spent another hour half-heartedly going through reports, his focus too shot for him to get much done, before he finally gave up and headed home, buying takeout along the way. He tried to put Casey's words out of his head because he didn't want to bring his irritation home to Jordan, but he ended up utterly failing.

"I know I don't have award-winning social skills," he blurted out as soon as Jordan opened the door for him, "but I'm not *that* terrible."

Jordan raised an eyebrow. "I agree?"

"I mean, isn't asking how autistic people make friends kind of rude?" Noah went on, as he set his backpack down, toed off his shoes, and stripped off his coat. "Google is a thing that exists. You don't have to talk to my face as though I'm some kind of alien. And so what if I don't like making jokes about my sex life?"

"Um...Noah?" A furrow had appeared between Jordan's eyebrows. "What are you talking about?"

Noah scrubbed his hands over his face. He knew he was doing that thing where he jumped between topics that were related in his mind and forgot to explain the connection to his listener. "Never mind. Forget I said anything. It's just O'Donnell being O'Donnell."

"Ah." Jordan's expression cleared. Noah had complained about Casey enough times before for him to get the picture.

Noah sat down with his dinner at the table while Jordan sipped at his mug with a dissolved blood pill. "How's the new boss?" Jordan asked.

Noah shrugged over his food. "She's a good leader, and she seems nice enough. Although..."

"What?"

"Her name is Ariel *Cross*. Interesting, huh?"

Jordan frowned. "Um...yeah, that is interesting, but it's probably a coincidence."

"True, although...she happened to transfer to our branch from Atlanta."

"Oh." Jordan averted his gaze, his expression unreadable to Noah. Jordan had lost contact with his family from a town near Atlanta decades ago, and it was something he still brooded over from time to time.

Noah fidgeted with his chopsticks. "Do you...want me to ask her about her family history?"

"It's...probably nothing," Jordan mumbled. "But...uh, if it comes up in conversation...maybe?"

"Wait." Noah nearly smacked himself on the forehead, pushed his takeout container aside, and got his laptop. "*Duh.* Why ask when you can Google?"

"Are you seriously searching her on the internet?" Jordan asked, sounding as though Noah had proposed breaking into her house.

"Why not? It's not like I'm going to stalk her Facebook or something. Besides, Rob mentioned something about the Cross family of vampire hunters, which I'd never heard of before."

"Huh," said Jordan. "I'd never heard of that either."

Noah's fingers flew over the keyboard, and he scanned the Google search results. "Okay...interesting. The Cross family of vampire hunters *is* kind of famous in the South, though they've only been around for a few generations. The founder, apparently, was Maryanne Cross—"

"*Wait.*" Jordan sounded choked. "Did you say *Maryanne Cross*?"

"Uh, yeah..."

Jordan stared hard at the table. "My sister's name was Maryanne Cross," he whispered.

Noah blinked. "Wait, so...your sister founded the Cross family of vampire hunters?" That sounded a bit too coincidental to really be a coincidence; he filed that away to wonder about later. "And you would be Ariel's... um...some kind of ancestor? Should I tell her?"

"No!" Jordan burst out, eyes wide with panic.

"Why not? If she's related to you, isn't that a good thing?"

"She's a vampire hunter from a family of vampire hunters." He folded his arms, shoulders hunching. "There's no way she wants to be related to me."

"*I'm* a vampire hunter, and I'm dating you," Noah pointed out.

The corner of Jordan's mouth pulled upward, but only for a brief moment. "Yeah, well...we took a while to get to that point, didn't we?"

"Yeah," Noah admitted. They weren't exactly an example of love at first sight. "But...I mean...you're a likable person. You have that friendly, polite Southern white boy charm thing going on."

Jordan gave a snort of laughter. "Seriously? You know I barely have the accent anymore."

"Hey, it worked on me."

Jordan rolled his eyes, though he was still smiling. "I'll...think about it, okay?"

"Okay." Not that Noah wanted to push Jordan or anything; he'd just thought reconnecting with his family might make Jordan happy.

And speaking of family...

Noah coughed. "By the way, I have my, uh...my thing on Sunday."

"Oh. Right." Jordan glanced away, clearing his throat. "I'll pick up an extra shift at the blood bank."

Noah hated the awkward atmosphere that permeated the space between them, but as usual, he wasn't sure what to do about it. It was the elephant in the room that neither he nor Jordan ever seemed to know how to deal with.

Noah swallowed down the lingering feelings of unease. "I'll see you after, all right?"

"Of course."

Jordan got up from his seat with his mug and made his way to the sink, but Noah intercepted him on the way there, tugging him close for a soft kiss. Jordan relaxed against him, and when he drew back, he gave Noah a small smile.

Hopefully, that was a good sign.

Sunday morning dawned bright and cold. Noah set off for the cemetery, his hands stuck into the pockets of the puffy winter coat that made him look like a red snowball, pausing to buy a bouquet of flowers from a grocery store along the way. He found Elsie already waiting at the entrance for him, carrying her own bouquet in her arms.

His elder sister was impeccably dressed, as usual, wearing a black trench coat, stylish scarf, and skinny jeans tucked into black boots. A red knitted beret covered her shoulder-length black hair. Although she often wore high heels when she went out, she always made sure to wear flats when she met with him—because the constant sound of high heels clicking on the ground drove him out of his mind—and for that, he was always grateful.

"Hey, bro," she said cheerfully. Way too cheerfully.

"It's cold," he grumbled in response after she hugged him.

"So?" Elsie grinned at him as they fell into step with each other, passing rows of tombstones. "How are things with Jordan?"

"Fine."

A moment of silence passed before she said, "You ever think of bringing him along?"

"Uh, why?"

She huffed out a breath. "Because you're the kind of person who usually wants to share every single part of your life with your significant other?"

Noah glanced away. "It's...awkward. You know. He's a vampire, Mom and Dad died because of a vampire..."

"Which is why you also haven't told Aunt Crystal about him yet?"

Noah grimaced. "I haven't told her about *every* person I've ever dated."

"Only the serious ones, and you're as serious about Jordan as I've ever seen you."

He gestured vaguely. "I just...I wouldn't know what to do if she got mad, being Mom's sister and all."

"You told *me*."

"Els, I literally couldn't sleep several nights before I told you I was dating Jordan," Noah pointed out. "I was afraid you were going to *disown* me."

She sighed. "I know you've had some really shitty experiences with other people, but I would never, *ever* disown you."

"I know," he said reluctantly.

"And neither would Aunt Crystal."

Sometimes, Noah hated the way his brain would latch on to past negative experiences with a death grip and never let go. His mental breakdown at the end of college—and all of the painful interactions he'd had—were a few years behind him, but they didn't feel far away enough for him to stop feeling anxious about the possibility of being rejected by other people.

He hummed instead of answering. Elsie walked beside him in silence for a while before asking, "Do you feel guilty about dating him?"

Noah bit his lip. Of course, trust the lawyer to get straight to the point.

"I don't feel *guilty*."

"But?" Elsie prompted.

Noah opened his mouth, closed it, and shrugged. "But nothing."

He suspected that she didn't believe him, but she didn't press him about it.

They'd reached their parents' gravestones. *In loving memory*, they read, followed by his parents' names: Joseph Lau and Jessica Lau. Noah crouched down to place his bouquet down as Elsie did the same. Sometimes they talked; today, they stood together in quiet contemplation.

Noah had been young when their parents had died, and he only had a few vivid memories to hold on to. Like dressing up for Halloween and giggling with Elsie while their dad insisted on taking pictures. Or watching Disney movies religiously with his mom until they both fell asleep on the couch. Or proudly talking about his parents for a school assignment, about how they were scientists who worked on ways to eradicate the vampirism virus.

Most of all, it hurt to think about all the what-ifs and might-have-beens. Whenever Noah accomplished something, like getting an A on a paper for school, and his parents weren't there for him to brag to. When he graduated from high school, and then from college, and his parents were never at the ceremonies. When his mental health fell apart and he spent long nights curled up in his dorm room bed, staring at his phone, not sure if he wanted to call Elsie or Aunt Crystal because he would just be a bother and wondering, if his parents had still been alive, would they have understood?

"Hey," said Elsie, softly.

"Hm?"

"I know we argued a lot when you became a hunter, but..." Elsie drew a breath. "I think Mom and Dad would be proud of you."

Noah blinked hard at that unexpected comment. "Th...thanks."

She turned to face him. "Whatever you do, whatever choices you make...you don't have to be scared of disappointing them, you know?"

"I know," he said, just because that was the simplest answer he could give. In reality, though, things weren't that simple. It was always a thought lurking in the back of his mind, questioning his choices, mocking him for his failures. It blended with the ableism he'd internalized throughout his life until he could no longer distinguish the two. His fears of being *not good enough* were always intertwined with *what would Mom and Dad think if they were still alive?*

It was why, even though Aunt Crystal was totally cool with him living with her after he'd graduated, and even though he could've saved some money that way, he couldn't bring himself to do it. It was why he still sometimes beat himself up over the fact that he didn't— *couldn't*—continue on to grad school. And it was why, sometimes when he couldn't sleep, he began to wonder what his parents, who dedicated their lives to eliminating vampires, would've thought of him dating Jordan—before his mind shut that train of thought down.

"That includes who you're dating," Elsie added. "You're going to have to introduce him to Aunt Crystal eventually, you know. It's almost the holiday season—and somehow I don't think you'd feel good about leaving Jordan out of our family gatherings."

She knew him way too well.

He sighed. "I told you, Els, I don't feel guilty."

"I know." She shrugged. "Just something to think about."

As far as Noah was concerned, there was nothing to think about. There was a paradox in his life, but he was fine just ignoring it. The one thing he *did* know was that, no matter what, he trusted Jordan with his life.

Chapter Six

SIX MONTHS EARLIER

Noah told himself that he only looked forward to Jordan's visits because Jordan was the one who brought him food, and also because his conversations with Jordan broke the monotony of being captive with no clear escape plan as of yet. Yet Jordan also remained an enigma, and even though Noah, by default, sucked at understanding other people, that didn't stop him from trying.

Although Jordan was always unfailingly polite, Noah couldn't shake the feeling that he was...sad, most of the time. He rarely smiled or laughed, and there was a strange heaviness in the way he spoke, sometimes. And questions about Julius only elicited evasive non-answers, which sorely piqued Noah's curiosity about their relationship.

Eventually, he worked out what he thought would be a non-obnoxious way to broach the topic. "How old is Julius?" he asked over a dinner.

Jordan blinked at him from where he was leaning against the adjacent wall. "I...I'm not sure. Several hundred years, I think. I tried to ask him a few times, but he said he'd been alive 'since the dawn of humanity,' and I have no idea what that actually means," he finished, his mouth twisting.

Noah knew that much from the initial tip to the VHA, though he was somewhat disappointed he couldn't get a more precise number. "How long have you been together?"

He'd meant it as an innocent question, but Jordan flinched as though Noah had hit him. He rested his head back against the wall, and for a moment, Noah thought he wasn't going to answer.

"Almost eighty years, I guess," Jordan finally said. His voice sounded strangely flat, expressionless.

"That's...a really long time," Noah said. It would've been impressive if not for the fact that Jordan didn't give off an obvious "immortal and happily in love" vibe. Given that Jordan had said he was born in 1921, Noah tried to do the math. "Did you meet him soon after becoming a vampire?"

Jordan shifted against the wall and didn't meet Noah's eyes. "He...he was the one who turned me."

"Oh." For some reason, the atmosphere suddenly felt awkward, though from what Noah knew, it wasn't uncommon for a vampire to turn their human lover.

Jordan stared at a point on the floor. "He didn't ask if I wanted to become a vampire before he did it."

"Oh," said Noah dumbly.

He'd known that, in theory, there were people who had been turned into vampires unwillingly, but since he'd only ever been concerned with vampires who attacked humans, he'd never thought much about them. Now that he was staring one in the face, he realized just how awful it was.

"Wow, I'm sorry," Noah added. "That must've really sucked."

Jordan grimaced, and Noah experienced a flash of paranoia. One of the problems with depending on memorized social scripts for his interactions was that people often thought Noah sounded insincere. He wasn't being insincere—most of the time—he just had problems with vocal inflection when he was reciting words from memory in the attempt to make a "socially appropriate" comment.

"I guess it was my fault," Jordan said, sounding bitter. "I was visiting my aunt and uncle in Atlanta at the time when I met him. He seemed so...I don't know, worldly and sophisticated. When I realized he knew that I was..." He fidgeted with his fingers for a long minute before stammering out, "that I was queer, I was scared. But he told me I had nothing to be ashamed of." He uttered a hollow laugh. "I was...infatuated. I couldn't believe someone like him would be interested in me, and I had this stupidly romantic idea that he'd come to rescue me from my life. So I ran away with him...before I learned he was a vampire and he'd turned me into one too, while I was sleeping."

Noah watched him, trying to slot the pieces of information together in his mind. Born in 1921. Visited family in Atlanta—presumably Atlanta, Georgia. Scared of other people knowing he was queer. He tried to imagine Jordan as a closeted teenager in 1930s Georgia, smitten with an older man who told him he didn't need to fear his desires.

"So...you lived in Georgia?" Noah asked.

Jordan nodded. "A small, rural town out of Atlanta."

"Religious?" Noah guessed.

"Awfully."

Wow, Noah thought, *that must've* really *sucked.*

"I thought you had kind of a Southern accent," he said.

Jordan's gaze flicked away. "It used to be much stronger."

"Oh?"

Jordan shrugged a little. "Julius didn't like it."

Noah didn't know what to say to that. It sounded...overly domineering to him. He didn't want to think that the entirety of their relationship was like that, because if that was the case, it was no wonder Jordan didn't seem happy. On top of the whole "literally never asked to be a vampire" thing.

"I'm...really sorry," he said. "For what happened to you."

"Thank you," Jordan said, softly. "That's kind of you to say."

After a pause, Noah asked, "So...you decided to move from Georgia to Massachusetts at some point?"

"We've been all over the country. Julius likes sticking near the big cities, especially New York. We moved here a few years ago."

That sounded interesting, but Jordan spoke without any obvious hint of excitement or passion.

Noah hesitated before asking, "Did you ever think of...leaving him?"

Jordan stared at him.

"I...no...if I left, where would I go? Besides, I didn't want to have to kill people for blood." He hunched his shoulders, as though he were trying to make himself seem smaller. "I mean, I know he killed them anyway, so it's not like I'm really innocent, but..."

Noah blinked. "You...didn't want to kill for blood?" Nowadays, there were vampires who swore they only got their blood from the blood pills, but he'd always taken it for granted that prior to the blood banks, all vampires happily went around going for people's jugulars.

Jordan tensed and hung his head. "I...if you don't believe me, I understand." His voice sounded broken and small. "But I...I never wanted this. I never wanted to hurt anyone."

Fuck. Jordan sounded so miserable that Noah didn't know what to do.

"But there are blood banks now," Noah said hesitantly. The blood banks had been set up by the government a few years ago, after a lot of political fights, due to the VHA and vampire rights groups uniting—for once—to argue that free blood would decrease the rates of vampire-on-human crime. "So you don't have to rely on him anymore for...um, you know."

"I know." Jordan hunched his shoulders. "It probably sounds stupid, but I guess...I'm scared that if I say it's over, then everything I gave up for him would've been for nothing, so what's the point of going on?"

Noah's insides lurched. Did...Jordan just admit he was suicidal?

"I...I'm sure there *is* a point," Noah said, the words sounding clunky and sluggish in his mouth. He'd always sucked at comforting people, even when he really did care for them. "Don't you have...hobbies? Things to look forward to? A life other than...him?"

Jordan looked away. "I don't know." His voice sounded unsteady. "I...used to have dreams, but it's been so long since I've...looked forward to anything." He closed his eyes. "I probably never could've achieved them, anyway."

Jesus Christ. What the hell had happened to Jordan's self-esteem? "I'm...I'm sure that's not true," Noah said, fumbling for words. "There are plenty of things to do...places to go...uh, books to read! Did you know there's an eighth Harry Potter book—as a play?"

Jordan blinked, slowly. "I never even got to read past the second book."

"Well, hey, you *have* to finish. And watch the new Batman movies, and...and...other things!"

Noah was babbling, but having experienced depression himself before, the thought of Jordan being depressed enough to consider suicide made him feel sick to his stomach.

Jordan didn't seem reassured; he curled in on himself even more tightly. "I'm sorry," he mumbled. "You're the one locked up in this room. I...I have nothing to complain about."

"Will you stop apologizing?" Noah's voice came out sharper than he'd intended, and he regretted it when Jordan flinched. "This isn't a contest for who has the shittiest life, okay? The situation I'm in sucks. What happened to you *also* sucks. You're allowed to complain."

"You don't understand. It's...it's my fault you're here," Jordan whispered. "And it's my fault your friends are dead."

"What do you mean?" Noah said, not following.

"I was the one who called the VHA." Jordan swallowed, blinking hard. "Julius, he...he was getting extreme with how many people he was killing. I wanted him to stop, but he wouldn't...he never listens to me. I wanted someone to stop him. I should've realized..." He covered his face with his hands, his voice breaking. "I'm so sorry."

Noah stared at him. He should've been angry at Jordan, and yet...he couldn't be.

"You didn't know," said Noah, awkwardly. "You were just...trying to do the right thing."

Jordan shook his head. "He's...he's killed so many, over the years. And for years, I did nothing. I mean, he's stronger than me, but...I...I should have done something." He blinked hard at the ground. "And I can't even figure out where he keeps the key for your shackle, and I—I'm such a useless coward. I'm sorry..."

Can't figure out where he keeps the key. Noah's lingering suspicion that Jordan still planned on drinking his blood faded. Unless Jordan was lying about that much...but then, why would he? He didn't have much to gain by playing on Noah's sympathy.

"You tried," Noah said, his tongue feeling awkward and clunky in his mouth. "That...counts for something."

Jordan shook his head again. "He's going to kill you," he whispered. "And I—I don't want you to die."

Noah blinked at him, heartbeat skipping in surprise. He looked at Jordan—Jordan, who didn't want to kill people for blood, who was crushed by guilt over having inadvertently led a group of hunters to death at Julius's hands, who'd been turned into a vampire without his consent.

"Maybe I won't die." But Noah's voice came out shaky, not confident.

Jordan's arms tightened around himself. Then, abruptly, he turned away.

"I'm sorry," he said again, his voice thick and unsteady. And then he fled.

Chapter Seven

When the alarm clock went off, slicing through Noah's sleep with the sound of a foghorn, Noah slammed the snooze button, cursing a blue streak in his slurred early morning mumble.

Jordan chuckled from behind him, arms wrapping around his waist. "Good Lord, Noah, what has that poor alarm clock ever done to you?"

I'm not awake yet, Noah wanted to say. Instead, he grumbled "Mmmphgrmph" as he settled back against Jordan's chest.

Jordan nuzzled his neck, and Noah hummed at the gentle touch, drowsy contentment slowly replacing his crankiness. They cuddled comfortably for a while, before Jordan pressed a kiss to Noah's nape and got up. Noah groaned, burying his head under the warm comforter, but he knew that was his cue that he had to get up for work. After a few more minutes of procrastinating, he dragged himself out of bed.

One mug of coffee later, he was feeling more awake as he perused the news while munching on toast.

> *HemRC, the Hemovore Rights Coalition, has once again asserted that the Vampire Hunters Association engages in willful execution of vampires, in violation of due process and human rights...*

"HemRC is in the news a lot these days, aren't they?" Jordan commented as he passed behind Noah before joining him at the table.

Noah put his phone down and sighed. "I'd love it if they could stop giving the VHA a bad name all the time," he grumbled. "It just makes our jobs harder."

The HemRC had somehow managed to move from a fringe group to an increasingly louder voice when it came to vampire—or "hemovore"—issues. The first time Noah had asked Jordan what he thought of the whole thing, Jordan had said, "I guess the name 'hemovore' is catchy, if you want to rebrand vampires as hipsters." Which made Noah snort out his tea.

Their platform mainly revolved around agitating against the VHA's elimination of vampires who attacked humans, claiming it as "inhumane" and "a violation of civil rights." They also worked to try to destigmatize vampirism in general and fight against perceived discrimination. The fact that they opposed the VHA made Noah automatically wary of them; the arguments had already been hashed out over and over again by people more eloquent than he—vampires were effectively immortal, which made the idea of building a vampire prison problematic, etc. etc.

"Do you think they'll cause serious problems for you guys?" Jordan asked. "They've been trending on Twitter more and more often lately."

"National polls indicate that most people in the US still support the VHA over the HemRC, and most people still think they're related to the vampire supremacists, which hurts their public image. But...I don't know." Noah sighed. He'd wondered the same thing himself. HemRC's increasing profile meant the VHA was getting more and more public criticism over the years, and he was worried that eventually it would all reach a boiling point.

"I'm with you," Jordan said, "but I know some people at the meetings are starting to think HemRC might have a point. There are rumors that peaceful vampires have been disappearing because of the VHA."

"Unless there's proof, rumors are only rumors," Noah scoffed. Having formerly worked in Investigations, he could say with confidence that the VHA vetted every vampire they targeted. Many of the vampires they went after were serial killers, drunk on their near-immortality and ability to overpower most humans.

The vampire who killed his parents had probably been one of those.

Noah went to get dressed. Jordan eyed him after he emerged from the bedroom. "Something going on today?"

Noah sighed. "Just...a team-building lunch with Ariel. I thought I should put a bit more effort into what I was wearing."

The only dress code for hunters was that they couldn't wear anything impractical to a hunt, so Noah's wardrobe for work consisted of jeans and T-shirts in the summer, and jeans, shirt, and fleece jacket in the winter. Unimaginative, but he didn't care as long as it was comfortable. Today, though, he actually dug out a gray button-down shirt and khakis.

Jordan smiled at him, that warm smile that seemed to reach inside Noah's chest and light a flame there, as his eyes did a down-up flick over Noah. "You look good."

"Thanks," Noah mumbled, pretty sure he was blushing. He cleared his throat. "It's just a lunch, so, whatever."

Jordan pecked him on the cheek. "Well, have fun."

The first oddity of the day: When Noah met up with the others for lunch, he found Ava and Ariel there, but not Casey.

"Where's O'Donnell?" Noah asked.

"Sick, apparently," Ava replied with a shrug. "His loss. We should take pictures of our food and text them to him to make him jealous."

"Sick for lunch with the new boss?" said Noah dryly. "I don't know, that sounds sketchy."

"I'll be sure to mention it in his annual review," said Ariel with a smile that indicated that she was probably just teasing. "Shall we?"

Rob joined them in the lobby, and they left the VHA building to head to a nearby Thai restaurant (which Noah was happy about, since he loved Thai food). After they ordered, the conversation kicked off with Rob asking Ariel about what it was like, growing up in a family of vampire hunters.

"I'm not sure what it's like for, say, the Van Helsings," Ariel said, "but for me, it was definitely the feeling of growing up listening to my parents' and grandparents' stories, and feeling like there was this legacy on my shoulders—a legacy that I wanted to live up to."

Ava immediately started talking shop with Ariel— how many elite hunts she'd been on, who her mentors were, what her tips were for dealing with elder vampires, etc. Noah listened along while chowing down on his Pad See Ew. Both the beauty and the drawback of group conversations was that he was bad at inserting himself into the conversation, since it often moved too quickly for him to both listen and come up with things to say at the same time.

"But that's enough about me," Ariel said at some point. "I'd love to hear more about you two. And our missing fourth party member."

Ava said, "Casey? Well, he's your regular career hunter, I guess. He joined the VHA because he thought hunting vampires would be more exciting than being a police officer or signing up for the army." She rolled her eyes a little. "He's not a complicated guy."

She was being charitable. When Casey wasn't around, Ava and Noah sometimes joked about him being the epitome of the Clueless Straight White Guy who said such tasteless things as "that's hot" when Ava mentioned she had a girlfriend and "How do you pick up Asian chicks?" to Noah (which Noah responded to by giving him a "pickup line" that was actually "fuck you" in Cantonese. When he'd admitted as much to Ava, she'd laughed and called him a menace).

Ava launched into her story, which Noah had heard before—how, when she'd been young, a vampire had preyed on the people who lived in the same public housing unit she and her family had been in, and that was how she'd been inspired to join the VHA.

"How about you, Noah?" Ariel said, turning her eyes to him during a lull in the conversation. "Tell me about yourself."

"Me?" Noah said, his face burning a little as he realized he was the center of attention. "Um…I'm not that interesting."

"Don't listen to him," Rob said, grinning. "He survived an attack by a several-hundred-year-old vampire and took him down all by himself."

Noah's face burned hotter. There were plenty of times when he regretted giving himself credit for what happened with Julius Saint Laurent at all. It felt dishonest, even if it had been a necessity, and he didn't want that kind of fame; he just wanted to do his job competently and fly under the radar. "That's not true," he blurted out. "The vampire was already seriously injured by the time I got there. I just shot him and ran off."

Rob chuckled. "He's very modest, our Noah," he told Ariel.

To Noah's relief, the conversation turned away from him again, and the others chatted pleasantly for the rest of lunch.

The rest of the day passed uneventfully enough until Noah received an email late in the afternoon—from Ariel.

Hi Noah,

Thanks for your hard work the other day. I'd like to talk to you for a few minutes in my office, if you're free. I don't have anything scheduled for the rest of the day, so feel free to stop by.

Best,

Ariel

Noah's heart knocked against his ribcage as he read the unexpected email. Was she talking to each member of their squad individually, or was he being singled out for some reason? Because of his disability? *No, don't be paranoid—I'm sure she's been talking to Ava and Casey too, just to get to know us. That's reasonable.*

Still, he couldn't quite shake his lingering nerves, his anxiety over not knowing what to expect, as he made his way to her office and knocked on the door.

"Come in," Ariel called out from inside.

Noah poked his head into Ariel's office. "You wanted to see me?"

Ariel smiled at him over the paperwork on top of her desk. "Yes, I did. Please close the door behind you, if you would, and have a seat."

Noah closed the door and sat in the chair in front of her desk. Ariel clasped her hands and regarded him.

"I read the report on the Saint Laurent incident. Very impressive for a rookie hunter," she said. "I'm surprised you didn't apply for becoming a squad leader after that."

Noah blinked, caught totally off guard by the comment. His mind had gone blank in surprise, but Ariel was still watching him, so he scrambled for something to say.

"Oh, uh...I don't know. I guess I still didn't think I was experienced enough. I got Saint Laurent mostly due to luck, but I could've died several times over. So, um, you know...I didn't think I was ready to be a squad leader yet."

Ariel nodded. Noah felt like he was taking some sort of test, and he hoped he'd passed so far.

"You seem to be a fairly by-the-books kind of guy," Ariel said, "and yet I hear you nearly lost your job over at Investigations. How'd that happen?"

Noah hesitated. He hated situations like these. Did Ariel want him to give her an honest answer, or was she laying a trap in case he badmouthed his former colleagues?

"I'm just curious," she added quietly. "I promise that whatever you say won't go beyond this room."

That could've been a lie, but Noah could only go so far in assuming everyone had an ulterior motive before he lost his mind. "I didn't have a good relationship with my boss in Investigations," he finally admitted. "She was looking for reasons to get rid of me."

Ariel raised an eyebrow. "From what I can tell, your work seems meticulous and your attitude reasonable. What was the problem between you and your former boss?"

Noah was beginning to sweat under his collar. He knew his diagnosis was listed in his file, but he was hesitant to bring it up in connection with his short-lived Investigations career. "Um...well, she just didn't like me very much," he said, weakly. "I never exactly figured out why."

"You never went to HR or anyone to talk to them about it?"

Noah swallowed. "I...didn't think they'd believe me. I didn't have proof that she disliked me because...because of a particular reason."

Ariel was still watching him. Noah began to fidget with the hem of his shirt, fingertips sliding over the smooth cotton. Pessimistic as he was, he began to wonder if Ariel had called him in because she wanted to fire him.

"I'd like to ask you about something, Noah," she said.

"Oh, uh...sure." She'd already been asking him questions, but whatever.

Ariel put a folder on her desk. "During the hunt, you mentioned that there had been issues with faulty intel on previous hunts. However, when I went through your case reports, I found no such references."

Noah blinked in disbelief. "That...that can't be right. I wrote those reports myself, and I *definitely* made a note of that..." He suddenly felt queasy. "You...don't think *I* messed up the reports, do you?"

She seemed to be studying his face. He dropped his gaze to the desk, away from her searching eyes.

"No," she said at last, "I don't believe so. But that just leaves the question of why what you said and what the reports said don't match up."

"I don't know," said Noah, helplessly. "I...I guess someone could've tampered with the reports after the fact? But I don't know who would do that, or why..."

She seemed to think for a moment, her gaze fixed on some faraway point. She took a breath, folding her hands on the desk. "I'd like to propose something. Something that I hope we can keep just between the two of us."

"Just the two of us?" Noah echoed. This was starting to sound somewhat shady. "Why not Ava and Casey?"

She pursed her lips. "Call it...cautiousness, for now. Would that be a problem?"

"Uh...no. You're the boss."

She gave him a small smile at that. "What I'd like you to do is go over these reports. See if there are any other discrepancies that you notice. If you see any, note what they are. Consider this as doing a personal favor for me."

"Okay." It struck him as tedious, but he wasn't going to argue with his new boss.

"Keep track of your hours, and I'll pay you out of my own pocket."

He blinked. "That's...very nice of you."

"I'm not trying to coerce free labor from you, I promise." She pushed the folder across the desk to him. "Start with these. Any questions?"

"Just to clarify: you don't want me to mention this to anyone else in the VHA, right?"

"Right. If you find something to worry about, then we'll find someone else to talk to. If not, we can save everyone else the worry." She smiled at him. "Thank you so much, Noah. I really appreciate this."

"No problem."

"So you won't believe what happened today," said Jordan when Noah got home from work.

"What?" Noah asked, thrown. "What happened?"

Jordan glanced at him. "Your coworker came by after I got home from my shift."

The words made no sense to Noah. "But how...who..." Then it dawned on him. "Wait...was it *Casey*?"

Jordan nodded.

There were so many things wrong with this scenario, Noah didn't even know where to begin. How did Casey figure out his address? Even if it was logged in an HR database somewhere, how could he have gained access to it? And, considering they never interacted outside of work and couldn't be considered friends, how the hell did Casey think it was okay to drop by his apartment without even asking Noah?

"What did he want?"

"I don't know. He said he was looking for you, and when I said that you were still at work, he just started...chatting with me, for a while?"

Noah's stomach churned with unease. "Did he peg you for a vampire, you think?"

"I don't know." Jordan's voice was soft, his brow furrowed. "He didn't say anything that made it seem like he was suspicious, but...I don't know. He was pretty nosy in general, like you've said." He looked away. "I...think he might suspect...you know. Us. He said something like, 'Roommates, is that what they're calling it these days?'"

Noah's heart sank, but that wasn't a total surprise. He gritted his teeth. "What is he, a *stalker*?"

Jordan fidgeted. "He's not...um...going to cause you trouble with your job...is he?"

Noah raked his hands through his hair. "I have no idea. I don't know if he's trying to look for something to blackmail me with, or what. Though I don't know why he'd even *want* to blackmail me in the first place." Sure, they weren't exactly BFFs, but neither did Noah ever get a sense of animosity from Casey.

Jordan hunched in on himself. "Could he blackmail you for being queer?"

"What? No—I don't think so." Sometimes Noah forgot how easily Jordan reverted to his fears of being out. "I don't really think that's blackmail-worthy at VHA Boston, thankfully."

Jordan blew out a breath. "Oh. That's—that's good."

Noah flopped down on the couch with a groan.

"Ugh. Too much bullshit from work. I need a nice, long, no-more-interacting-with-people vacation."

"Hey, what about me?" Jordan asked, his tone light enough to be teasing.

"You're not 'people,' you're 'very important people.' You're exempted, of course."

"Of course."

He could hear the smile in Jordan's voice before Jordan leaned down to kiss him. They lay in a comfortably tangled heap on the couch, Jordan's weight a soothing pressure against Noah's chest.

"What else happened at work?" Jordan murmured.

Noah explained Ariel's request. By the time he'd finished, they were sitting upright on the couch, and Jordan was frowning at him.

"So, let me get this straight," said Jordan. "Your new boss decided to give you extra clerical work to do because...she thought you wouldn't complain?"

"Do you have to put it that way?" Noah sighed. "She said it was because I'm trustworthy."

"She was just trying to make you feel good about getting an extra workload," Jordan grumbled.

As much as Noah hated to admit it, Jordan was probably right. This was why he needed a personal translator for conversations with allistics. "I mean, there *is* a problem with the reports, but I'm not sure what *I* can do about it other than correct them. I can't really figure out who might've altered them..."

Jordan settled back against the couch. "Why would anyone do that, anyway?"

"My best guess? To erase the evidence of their own incompetence for screwing up intel, so they can't be blamed for it if it ever comes up." Noah rolled his eyes. "Now I'm the unlucky bastard who's trying to untangle this whole mess."

Jordan made a sympathetic sound. "Anything I can do to help?"

Noah's growing annoyance immediately flipped into warm, gooey feelings of gratitude. He grinned at Jordan. "Give me a motivational kiss?"

"I meant with your paperwork," Jordan protested, but he leaned over obligingly to press his lips to Noah's in a soft, far-too-fleeting kiss.

"Nah, I'm probably good. Thanks for offering, though." Although it did feel like busywork, Noah didn't mind mundane tasks that required an eye for detail too much.

Jordan sighed. "Now I see why you complain about overtime," he muttered.

"I'm sure it won't be that bad," said Noah, trying not to make him worry. "I'm pretty sure we'll have to hand this over to HR, anyway. They'd know what to do about something like this."

"Sounds good to me." Jordan pressed his cheek to Noah's shoulder. "You work too hard, anyway."

"Not really," Noah mumbled, though a warm feeling bubbled up in his chest.

Jordan smiled. "I know something that'll help you relax."

"Yeah?"

He rummaged underneath the coffee table and brought out a DVD case. "Your favorite movie about saving the world with giant robots."

Noah's heart jumped. "Oh, *yes*. Absolutely." He took the DVD from Jordan's hand and looked at him. "Would you ever co-pilot a giant robot with me to save the world?"

A slow smile spread across Jordan's face, so infectious that Noah found the corners of his own mouth turning up.

"Absolutely."

Grinning, Noah threw his arms around Jordan, kissing him on the mouth.

Chapter Eight

SIX MONTHS EARLIER

Noah pulled at the end of his chain attached to the bed post. He'd gone back to his plan of trying to weaken the post from the bed frame—all four inches thick of it. He'd probably succeed in...maybe a year or two.

Jordan hadn't shown up that day yet, and Noah tried not to feel worried or uneasy about it. Ever since the long conversation they'd had about how Jordan became a vampire, he'd become quiet around Noah again. And Noah had to admit...it hurt. It was bizarre to think of Jordan as almost a friend, but Noah hadn't had that long of a conversation with anyone about non-work stuff, other than his sister and aunt, for a long time.

Well. Not that most people wanted to be friends with Noah, anyway. Sooner or later his weirdness got to be too much for them.

He pushed that thought aside and yanked at the chain again, stifling a curse as the impact jarred his leg. Just then, the door opened, and Jordan scurried in.

"I have the key," Jordan said breathlessly.

Noah blinked at him, his mind slow to catch up. "The key?" he echoed.

Jordan knelt by Noah's ankle and fiddled with the lock. The shackle loosened a moment later. Noah gaped at him.

"I found out where he'd been keeping it." Jordan smiled a little, though he then ducked his head. "I'm sorry it took so long."

"Sorry?" Noah repeated, stunned. "You *found* it. Seriously, you have absolutely nothing to be sorry for."

Jordan held a hand out to him and pulled him to his feet. "Come on. Julius left the house, so you have time to escape."

Noah followed him unsteadily out of the room, his legs wobbly after weeks of little movement. He almost wondered if he were dreaming; everything felt so surreal. "What about you?" he asked.

"Me?" Jordan turned wide eyes to him. He lowered his gaze. "I...I'll be fine."

Noah's heart clenched painfully. *Bullshit*, he wanted to say. *You're miserable here. Even I can tell that much.* "Come with me," he said softly.

Jordan shook his head, biting his lower lip. "I can't. He'd—"

He suddenly stiffened, head jerking up, nostrils flaring.

"Oh, no," he whispered.

"What?" Noah asked, tensing. "What is it?"

Without warning, Noah was swept off his feet, wind rushing against his face, before he abruptly found himself in what appeared to be the kitchen. His disoriented mind took a minute to catch up. Holy fucking hell, had Jordan just picked him up and whisked him down the stairs like he weighed nothing?

"He's back," Jordan breathed, eyes wide. "I don't know why. You have to run! I'll stay and—"

A cold voice stopped them both. "Jordan, I am so disappointed in you."

Standing in the kitchen doorway was Julius Saint Laurent. Noah hadn't paid attention before, but now he realized that Julius towered over Jordan—he must've cleared six feet, while Jordan was about Noah's height, five foot seven. Jordan cringed, shoulders hunching as he slowly turned to face him. He reminded Noah of a sprouting plant, shriveling up in the face of an arctic blast.

Noah's eyes darted around. He spied a collection of knives on the kitchen counter. This was probably the worst idea he'd ever had, but it was also his last chance to escape. He lunged for one of the knives—

He didn't even make it before he was knocked down, his head thudding painfully against the wooden cabinets. He groaned.

"Don't!"

Jordan's voice. Noah blinked, trying to push past the sharp ache in his skull. Julius was in front of him, one hand grasping a fistful of Noah's jacket.

"Don't!" Jordan pleaded. "Julius, don't. Please. You killed the rest of the hunters; Isn't that enough?"

Julius let go of Noah and turned to Jordan. Jordan shrank back.

"Why?" Julius sneered. "Do you fancy him? Wish to *fornicate* with him? *He* can get your blood up, but *I* can't?"

It was probably an inappropriate thought at the moment, but Noah couldn't help thinking: *Who the hell says "fornicate"?*

Jordan's jaw clenched. "That's not what this is about," he said, his voice surprisingly steady. "This hunter—he's weak. He can't hurt you. Can't you just let him go?"

"You and your squeamishness again. You've been a vampire for nearly eighty years, and yet you still refuse to feed." Julius sighed. "What am I supposed to do with you, Jordan?"

Jordan's gaze dropped to the floor. "I didn't *ask* for this," he said, his voice small. "You never gave me a choice."

"Why must you still cling to your memories of humanity, when we are so much more?" Julius gripped Jordan by the shoulder and shoved him down onto the floor in front of Noah. "*You* kill him."

Jordan's hands curled into fists. "No," he whispered. "I won't."

"What was that?" Julius said, his voice sharpening.

Jordan turned to face him. "I *won't kill him*," he repeated.

Julius stared at him. Then, he seized the collar of Jordan's shirt. "I should've locked you up in a room with the hunter," he said, his voice cold. "See how long you lasted then."

Jordan recoiled, his already pale face going bone white. "No—don't—please," he stuttered, his voice broken.

Julius let go of his shirt with a sigh. "Why do you always do this to me, Jordan? Make me be the villain? I don't like hurting you; you know that. I just want us to be happy again. Do you remember?"

Jordan looked down, sniffling. "I remember," he mumbled.

Noah felt sick. If this was how Julius always talked to Jordan, it was no wonder Jordan spoke as though he needed to apologize for the air he used. *Don't listen to him, he's manipulating you!* he wanted to shout.

"So just do this one thing for me," Julius said, his voice soft now. "If you love me, you'll do this for me. Please, Jordan."

Jordan wiped his sleeve across his face. "If *I* love you?" he echoed, his voice shaking. Angry, Noah thought. "When have you ever listened to *me*?"

"Don't be so childish," said Julius.

"You're the one who left me stuck as a nineteen-year-old forever," Jordan snapped back.

"Yes," said Julius, his mouth curling, "all the youth of a nineteen-year-old, and yet you've only ever had the stamina of a ninety-year-old."

Jordan blanched, his expression crumpling as though Julius had just hit him again. Noah felt like he'd missed something in the conversation, but just seeing that awful pain on Jordan's face made him want to stake Julius in the heart.

Noah made one last desperate pass at the kitchen knives, but he couldn't even pull himself up to the counter before Julius grabbed him and threw him to the opposite side of the room. His back collided against the cabinets again, knocking the wind from his lungs.

"Pathetic hunter," Julius said, his voice cold, fangs elongated and gleaming in his mouth. "You're nothing but a maggot."

Noah was going to die. Just like his parents had.

His life didn't flash before his eyes; his thoughts dissolved into pure terror.

I'm going to die I'm going to die I'm going to—

Julius suddenly gasped and jerked, the tip of a knife emerging from his throat. He crumpled to the ground. Jordan stood behind him, a long kitchen knife in his hands.

Before Julius could recover, Jordan crouched down and plunged the knife all the way through his neck again, with enough force to sever his head from his body.

Noah sucked in harsh, panting breaths, feeling dizzy with shock. He was almost certain that he was hallucinating in the second before Julius killed him.

His hand curled on the hard linoleum floor. This...didn't feel like a hallucination, though.

I'm...alive? Julius...is dead? What...the fuck?

There was a clattering sound as Jordan's knife slipped from his hand and landed on the floor, loud as a gunshot in the stillness of the kitchen. Jordan sank to his knees and covered his face with his hands, a sob escaping through his fingers.

Noah blinked as reality sank in and his body slowly slid out of fight-or-flight mode. His heart ached as he watched Jordan, but he didn't know what to say to comfort him. *Thanks for saving my life, and don't feel too bad about killing your lover of more than seven decades since he was a major asshole anyway* didn't seem to cut it.

Jordan raised his head, his face smeared with Julius's blood. His tongue darted out to lick some of it from his lips, and Noah tried not to flinch. "Will you kill me?" he whispered.

Noah recoiled. "What? No! The VHA—we only target vampires who kill people."

"But I have." More tears spilled out over Jordan's face and mingled with the bloody smears. "I've k-killed people. H-he made me..." He lowered his head.

Fuck.

Noah sat there, frozen. He'd never considered that Jordan might've killed people; he didn't think it was possible given how much Jordan loathed the bloodsucking part of being a vampire. But even Jordan couldn't be immune to the blood thirst.

Any vampire who ever killed a human was a target for the VHA.

And yet, as Noah looked at the vampire who'd saved his life, who knelt on the ground to await his judgment...he realized he couldn't do it.

"I'm not going to kill you," he said, his voice coming out harsh.

Jordan raised his head, brow furrowed. "What?" he croaked.

Noah tried to come up with the words to explain, but it had been an absolutely fucking *exhausting* day, and he was running out of energy to monologue.

"Do you have a phone?" he asked, his voice hoarse with fatigue.

Jordan stared at him. "Um..." After a minute, he inched toward Julius's body and fumbled with his pockets before taking out a smartphone. "Uh...it's locked, though. I don't...know the passcode."

Of course. "What about you?" Noah asked.

"Um. One second." Jordan shuffled out of the kitchen. He returned a second later with...*Oh my God,* Noah thought, horrified, *is that a candy bar phone from like 2000?*

"Are you kidding me?" he asked.

Jordan flinched. Noah hadn't meant to sound hostile, but...well, that was the story of his life. He tended to lose control over his vocal inflection when he was tired. "I'm sorry. It's all I have."

Noah leaned his head back. "No, sorry...I just wanted to be able to text, that's all."

"You can text with it, it just...uh...takes a while," said Jordan, in a small voice.

Well, that was better than nothing. Noah took the phone from Jordan and, using the keypad, painstakingly composed a text message to Rob at the VHA:

This is Noah Lau. Julius St Laurent is dead. Please send extraction. He asked Jordan for the address of the house and entered it.

Before he hit the button to send, Noah turned to Jordan. "You can't stay here. Where are you going to go?"

Jordan stared back at him. "I..." He swallowed hard. "I don't know."

Noah thought for a second before pulling his wallet out of his pocket and tossing a twenty-dollar bill at him. "Here. Take the commuter rail downtown to Medford. I'll meet you at the T stop near where I live."

Jordan was still staring at him. "What? But...I couldn't..."

"I'm asking for an extraction. You'd better get out of here before the VHA arrives. If you don't have anywhere else to go, you can crash at my place for a few days. Okay?"

"I...okay," Jordan whispered. He made his way to the backdoor and paused, giving Noah one last look before he left.

Noah sent the text. He scooted as far away from Julius Saint Laurent's decapitated corpse as he could and settled in to wait for the extraction.

It had been a hell of a day.

Chapter Nine

"O'Donnell. What the *hell*."

Casey blinked at Noah over his morning coffee. "Good morning to you too, Lau."

"You looked up my address and *came to my apartment* yesterday. So, again: What the hell?"

"Jeez, relax. Do you greet all of your friends like this?"

We're coworkers, not friends, Noah had to bite his tongue to keep himself from saying.

"I just wanted to hear about how the lunch went. I was super pissed that I got a stomach bug from the seafood place I went to the night before and had to spend most of the day at home instead of with you guys."

Noah frowned. "And you couldn't wait to ask me until today because...?"

"I was in the area, so I decided to drop by and ask. I messed up your schedule, obviously. And before you start accusing me of being a stalker, Lucy was the one who passed your address on to me in case of an emergency."

Noah kept frowning. The idea that Lucy Choi, their former squad leader, had done that was paternalistic and rude. He didn't want to believe it since he'd liked Lucy, though he couldn't really ask her since she'd moved to VHA Central.

"Don't worry," Casey drawled. "I won't tell anyone you're gay."

He said, while they were standing in the public break room with the door open to the hallway. Noah wanted to go over and bang his forehead against the door.

"I'm not gay," Noah said, inwardly seething.

Casey raised an eyebrow. "Right. The 'roommates' thing?"

"Believe it or not, O'Donnell, there are more sexual orientations than just 'gay' and 'straight'." And with that, Noah returned to his cubicle before he got pissed off enough to say something he would later regret.

In the meantime, he still had his side assignment from Ariel to worry about. He steadily made his way through his stack of reports. Some of them had been altered compared to what he remembered; some of them he wasn't sure about, and some of them he was pretty sure had been left alone. But aside from the missing comments about inaccurate intel, he wasn't sure if the reports had any other problems.

He hashed out a meeting time with Ariel over email and knocked on the door to her office right before lunch. After closing her office door behind him, he sat in front of her desk and reported his progress as she listened, hands clasped under her chin.

Ariel didn't respond right away. When she finally spoke, she said, "Did you find anything else that the tampered reports had in common? Like, say...anything about the vampire targets?"

"Um..." Noah racked his memory but couldn't think of anything off the top of his head. "Not that I remember..."

"I'd appreciate it if you took another look. It seems hard to believe that this is happening at random."

Noah blinked. "Wouldn't the answer just be that someone in Investigations is being sloppy, but aggressive about it? Like, they're supplying inaccurate information and then covering up their tracks by erasing any comments about it?"

"Possible," said Ariel, shrugging, "but we should also consider other options besides just 'aggressive' sloppiness."

"Like what? Wait." His thoughts caught up to him. "Are you saying that this is all some sort of...conspiracy?"

She raised an eyebrow. "Well, what do you think, Noah?"

She sounded neutral rather than condescending—at least, as far as Noah could tell. He clenched and flexed his suddenly sweaty fingers in his lap, his face feeling hot under her gaze.

"I...uh...I guess it's kind of suspicious," he mumbled. "But—but the whole purpose of VHA Investigations is to make sure we're going after actual vampires who pose a threat to humans. If someone is purposefully making up the information instead of investigating, then what's the point? We might as well pack up and say HemRC is right about us." He frowned. "Although...how could someone do something like this without anyone else noticing? Investigations has strict verification protocol."

"That's what I was thinking," Ariel agreed. "That's why I'm afraid that this could be the work of multiple people under a ringleader. Possibly even a rogue faction."

Noah's head began to swim. He didn't want to believe this was true. He'd joined the VHA because he believed in justice—because he hadn't wanted any other child to lose their parents to a vampire attack the way he had. But justice didn't mean indiscriminately killing vampires either.

"That's...a little extreme, isn't it?" he said nervously. "Shouldn't we talk to HR or Director Bellamy if that's the case?"

Ariel pursed her lips. "I'd like to try to see if there's a reason those particular reports were tampered with, and if we can figure out who might be behind it before we try talking to someone higher up."

"Okay," Noah said, trying not to sound too reluctant. He hesitated. "Um...how am I supposed to figure out who did this? I can't exactly go into Investigations and start asking people, especially since whoever it is has been trying to cover up the evidence."

Ariel's desk phone rang. "Just try to find out what you can. Every little bit of information helps. We'll continue this conversation later," she said before she answered the phone.

He slunk out of her office, feeling like he'd just been dumped in over his head.

Noah was slowly losing his mind.

The vampires mentioned in the tampered reports didn't seem to have anything in common with one another: not age, race, gender, or place of residence.

He read the reports over and over until his eyeballs felt like they were melting in his sockets. Then, he took out his frustration in the VHA's indoor gym, hoping some inspiration would come to him while he sweated his way through a workout.

Maybe it wasn't about the vampires themselves, but who they were associated with?

By the time he returned to his desk, it was late in the day. Normally, he'd clock out at this hour, but he wanted to make one last pass to test out his new hypothesis before calling it quits for now.

He texted Jordan that he would be home late and began examining the lists of human victims on the tampered reports.

The problem wasn't obvious, and he normally would've chalked it up to more sloppiness, but now that he was paying attention, it was staring him in the face: none of the victims in the tampered reports had any morgue or living relatives listed under their names.

Standard Investigations protocol dictated that investigators had to put down as much information as possible regarding the victims, as there had been one notorious case in the VHA's history in which a human serial killer faked vampire attacks on his victims, and the victims' bodies had to be re-examined. Again, the investigator in charge of the reports either got lazy and didn't bother...or there was a more sinister reason.

So the question was: were most of the victims...not even real?

It was a horrible thought, but Ariel's paranoia had rubbed off on Noah. Out of desperation, he began Googling the names.

By the time his internet browser was crammed full of tabs, Noah began to relax. He'd managed to turn up missing persons reports that matched the names he'd searched up, and he'd easily found the names of the victims' family members through the police database the VHA had access to. But that just made it even stranger that the reports were incomplete.

He then scanned the information regarding the witnesses who'd reported the vampire attacks on the victims and frowned. Oddly, one witness name turned up several times: Darryl O'Brian. A Google search revealed that he owned a bar. Why would that be the site for multiple vampire attacks?

Noah wasn't even close to figuring the puzzle out, and he didn't think he was going to get any more information regarding the victims. The only other option he could think of was to track down the victims' families and this Darryl O'Brian question them in person—an idea that filled him with dread.

He wished that he could at least push that task off for a week or so, but unless a last-minute hunt came in, tomorrow was the best day for him to skip coming in to headquarters.

Noah leaned back in his chair with a groan and rubbed his eyes as he glanced at an office window. It was already dark outside, and the hunter night shift had started. He grabbed his stuff, logged off on his computer, and headed home.

He arrived to find his apartment filled with the kind of New Age-y music Jordan listened to whenever he wanted to relax.

"Oh, hey." Jordan turned down the volume as he got up from the couch. His brow crinkled. "You look exhausted."

Jordan was one of the few people who could apparently read his face, while most people seemed to think Noah was as expressive as a sheet of paper.

Noah massaged the bridge of his nose, sighing. "Just work stuff. Racking up those overtime hours." He made his way to the fridge to fish out some leftover chasiu bao for dinner, which he popped into the microwave. "Oh, and Casey is an ass."

"You talked to him?"

"Yeah. Sort of." Noah rolled his eyes. "He tried to act all buddy-buddy even though I have no idea in what universe we'd count as friends." He was still suspicious of O'Donnell, but he figured he wouldn't be able to wrangle anything else out of him.

"Weird," Jordan commented as he slid into the seat across from Noah at the kitchen table. "How's the side project?"

"Frustrating." Noah wasn't sure he wanted to share Ariel's suspicions with Jordan yet. Not because he didn't trust Jordan, but because he didn't want to believe it himself. And, well...Jordan had never taken issue with Noah being a vampire hunter, probably because Jordan himself had some deep-seated issues with vampires, but Noah still didn't feel good saying, "Hey, what *if* the VHA is killing innocent vampires, though?"

"Sorry to hear that." Jordan clasped his hands on the table. "Wish there was something I could do to help."

Even though he had a mouth full of bao, Noah felt himself smile. Probably awkwardly. He should be used to Jordan's moments of sweetness by now, but he didn't think he'd ever take them for granted. He swallowed and said, "It's okay. Thanks for offering, though." After chewing another mouthful, he asked, "How was your day?"

Usually, nothing exciting happened at Jordan's part-time job at the blood bank, but this time, he shifted restlessly. "Well...there was almost a fight in the lobby this morning."

Noah frowned. "Over what?"

"The same rumors about disappearing vampires, and people saying the VHA is to blame."

Shit. Appetite abruptly gone, Noah put down the last bit of bao he had left.

"Sorry," Jordan murmured. "It's just their opinion."

"Yeah," Noah forced himself to say. "Do you think the rumors might be...coming from somewhere, though? I mean...think about HemRC. They hate the VHA, sure, but they usually don't make things up."

Jordan blinked. "I don't know. Vampires often 'disappear' if they think their neighbors are getting suspicious, in the sense that they pack up and leave. And vampires aren't always peaceful toward one another either."

"Okay, but if someone decides to leave town—like Amy—wouldn't they at least let their friends know?"

Jordan frowned. "I guess..."

Sometimes, Noah wished his brain would shut up. He rubbed his forehead, exhaling hard.

"Hey." Jordan's voice was low, soothing. "I'm sure there's some other reason she hasn't been around."

"You're not worried?" Noah asked. "She *is* your friend...or at least, a person you've seen a lot at the meetings..."

"I *am* worried, but not worried that the VHA had anything to do with it." Jordan tilted his head to the side. "Unless...you think they *are* involved?"

Noah shook his head. "They can't be," he said. Ariel had to be wrong. He'd worked in Investigations for almost a year. He *knew* how the VHA worked and the principles they lived by.

"I believe you," said Jordan.

Noah leaned his elbows against the table and blew out a slow breath. "I feel like my mind's going screwy from everything that's happened lately."

Jordan's eyebrows knitted. "I'm sure it'll blow over."

Noah nodded. At least, he hoped so. He hoped all of Ariel's paranoia was for nothing and life could go back to normal. He sighed and finished his bao.

"I don't want to work tomorrow," he grumbled as he brought his plate over to the kitchen sink.

"Take a sick day."

"Wish I could, but then I'd just be postponing what I have to do to another day."

"That bad, huh?" Jordan got up from his seat and leaned against the counter as Noah rinsed his plate. He gently nudged Noah with his elbow. "We could do something nice tomorrow night to unwind."

"Something nice?" The thing was, they couldn't splurge on a fancy meal, since Jordan didn't eat. And, as they were both introverts, their idea of relaxation was, by default, hanging out on the couch and watching movies or playing video games. "Like...?"

Jordan shrugged. His mouth curled into a half smile that made Noah want to kiss him. "Maybe it'll be a surprise."

"Oh, that is *so* unfair," Noah muttered as he dried his hands.

Jordan pressed a fleeting tease of a kiss to his lips. "It'll give you something to look forward to."

Noah huffed, but he couldn't quite help smiling. "Fine. It's a date, then."

Chapter Ten

SIX MONTHS EARLIER

The VHA medics insisted on keeping Noah in the infirmary overnight, even though he told them that all he needed was an ice pack for his throbbing head. During his stay, Rob dropped by to give him an awkward hug.

"I never should've assigned you to that squad," Rob kept saying. "Your sister nearly killed me. We were all worried sick."

Right. Noah was going to have to call Elsie at some point soon. He dreaded the inevitable confrontation, knowing she'd been against him becoming a hunter from the start.

"So." Rob cleared his throat. "I know you've just been through a harrowing experience, and probably the last thing you want to do is talk about it, but...how *did* you end up defeating that vampire all on your own?"

Noah had thought hard about how to answer that question while he'd been waiting for the VHA's extraction and on the way back to Boston. He was wary of hinting at Jordan's existence, but he also thought it would be pretty unbelievable if he said he took down Julius all by himself. In the end, he went for a mix.

"I got really lucky," he said. "There was...another vampire that visited him one day, and I thought I heard them fighting. I managed to escape the room I'd been held in through a window, and I saw that the vampire—Saint Laurent—was heavily injured. So I finished the job."

"Hm." Rob's expression was somber. "You're lucky you survived, after what happened to Jespersen and the rest."

"Yeah," Noah said, his mouth dry. "They didn't...did any of them..."

"Make it out?" Rob shook his head.

"Oh." Noah's stomach twisted. It had been a long shot, but he'd still hoped some of them had survived.

"So..." Rob gave him a weak smile. "Are you in the middle of packing your bags?"

It took Noah a minute to realize what Rob meant. "I still need to pay the rent."

Rob chuckled, as though Noah had made a joke, although he'd been completely serious.

"Well, consider yourself on leave for the rest of the week. When you come back, we'll talk about putting you on administrative leave while you recover."

"Thanks," said Noah, giving him a grateful smile.

As soon as the doctors released him, he picked up his phone from where he'd left it in his work locker, sighing when he powered it on and saw that Elsie had blown up his phone with frantic texts. Rob had probably told her already, but he typed a quick reply anyway—*Back now, I'm fine, will explain later*—and then left the VHA to collect Jordan from the T stop. He was nervous that Jordan had already left, given that Noah hadn't showed up when he said he would, but luckily, he found Jordan there, sitting on one of the benches.

"Sorry for making you wait so long. The VHA doctor made me stay the night just in case I had a concussion."

"Are you okay?" Jordan asked.

"I'm fine. Let's just go—"

Noah stopped, a thought occurring to him. He pivoted slowly back to face Jordan. "You...haven't had...I mean, you haven't *fed* in a while, have you?"

He thought Jordan turned a shade paler. "I can last another day," he said after a pause, his voice very quiet. "Maybe two."

Right. Well, the absolute last thing Noah wanted to deal with was a starved vampire on his hands. "Let's stop by the blood bank before we get back, then."

He looked up the location on his phone and hopped on the T downtown. Noah had never actually seen the blood bank before, and he wouldn't have been able to tell from the outside. It appeared to be a perfectly ordinary office building, and it was only when they entered that he saw the signs and the reception area.

He wondered if it was a complicated procedure to receive blood pills, but no; all the staff did was register Jordan's information and then hand him a bag that they said would last him a week.

After they got off the T at the stop closest to Noah's place, Jordan examined his bag. "Whoever invented these deserves a Nobel prize. I never would've thought people would establish free blood banks for vampires." He shook his head. "Then again, I never would've predicted the internet either."

"It was politically very unpopular for a while," Noah said. He'd read about the arguments with interest. "There were some people who said providing free blood would make more people *want* to become vampires. In the end, though, the mandatory vaccination, combined advocacy by the VHA and HemRC, and some data by social science researchers convinced Congress that blood banks would reduce homicides. And the data since then proved it, over and over."

"I guess that makes sense," said Jordan, quietly. "And...no increase in the number of people...*trying* to become vampires?"

"Um...well, it's been hard to measure," Noah admitted. "Plus, there are multiple factors involved. Like the rise of vampire supremacists and vampire junkies, some of whom actively try to convince people not to take the vaccine and become vampires instead."

Jordan shuddered. "*Why?*"

"Because they want immortality?" said Noah, bitterly. "Apparently there was a rash of people who rushed to become vampires after it became public knowledge, until the vaccine was developed and became mandatory."

"I remember." Jordan looked away. "Julius wasn't happy about all those people."

Noah fell silent. It was the first time Jordan had brought up Julius since, well, he'd killed him, and Noah didn't know whether he was supposed to brush it aside or not.

"I thought he would've liked having new vampires around," he said hesitantly.

Jordan laughed. It wasn't a happy-sounding laugh.

"He...had some weird ideas about vampires. He said it was a 'gift,' only to be bestowed on the 'worthy,' not on the 'riffraff.' Whatever that was supposed to mean."

Noah had never heard Jordan sound so disdainful before. "Yikes. Sounds like the vampire supremacists."

Jordan shrugged and seemed to let the conversation die. That was probably Noah's cue to move on to something else, or just stay silent, but curiosity kept gnawing away at the back of his mind.

He cleared his throat. "So...I'm just curious, but um...given that you spent, uh, a hell of a lot of time around him, how come you never believed in his philosophies?"

Jordan's brow furrowed at the sidewalk. "I think...um..." His hand crept up and absently rubbed the side of his neck. "I always had a hard time 'letting go' of my...humanity. It was something he used to criticize me for a lot. Maybe it was because he never gave me a choice about becoming a vampire." He shrugged a little, looking away. "Also, as time went on, I realized that he was wrong about a lot of things. So...it became easier to believe that his beliefs about vampires could be wrong, too."

"What do you mean?" Noah asked.

"Um...well..." Jordan glanced at Noah briefly. "He was pretty racist."

"Oh." Not that that was really a surprise, after the "Oriental" comment.

"And sexist." Jordan bit his lip and sighed. "And, I mean...I told you about when and where I grew up. By today's standards, *everyone* was prejudiced back then. Even I...I'm not proud of the things I used to believe, but...I've been trying to do better."

Noah had wondered about that. He took it as a good sign that Jordan at least recognized that racism and sexism were actual things.

They reached Noah's apartment building. He led Jordan up the stairs to his unit, unlocked the door, and held it open for Jordan to follow him inside.

"So...yeah, this is where I live," said Noah, gesturing vaguely at the kitchen and living area with a couch and TV. Compared to Julius's mansion, his tiny one-bedroom apartment was like a matchbox, but if Jordan was unpleasantly surprised, he didn't say anything. "You can stay as long as you need, until you find a friend to crash with or something."

"Oh." Jordan seemed to deflate. "Right. I...I'll try to get out of your way soon."

Oh, crap, Noah thought. "I didn't...I wasn't trying to kick you out right away or anything. I don't really mind. I just thought, um...you'd rather stay with a friend."

Jordan studied the ground. "I...don't really have any friends," he said, his voice barely above a whisper.

Well...shit.

Noah knew what *that* felt like, even though he was surprised to hear Jordan say that. Jordan, as far as he could tell, was not autistic, and he seemed to have a pleasant enough personality. Unless... Julius was the reason he didn't have any friends?

Pushing that unsettling thought to the side for now, Noah said, "Oh, well...then you can hang around here, I guess. As long as you're quiet and not too messy, and if you don't mind sleeping on the couch...and, I mean, if you're okay rooming with a hunter," he added awkwardly.

Jordan glanced at him. "I'd be kind of a hypocrite if I had a problem with you killing vampires," he said softly.

Noah opened his mouth, then closed it. *Ah, hell.* Was there *any* way to make this conversation *not* awkward? "Isn't that kind of...different?" he said, aware that he was probably only digging himself into a deeper hole. "I mean...doesn't my job bother you? At all?"

Jordan gave Noah a look that he couldn't read. "Doesn't it bother you that I'm a vampire? That I could kill you in your sleep?"

Noah stared at him. "Wow, you really suck at giving sales pitches."

"It's true," Jordan murmured. "The way I see it, you have more reason to be scared of me than I have reason to be scared of you."

"I didn't mean you should be scared of me, I meant...you know...I hunt...your kind." That phrase had never sounded as awkward as when Noah said it at that moment. "Doesn't that make you uncomfortable, like, on principle?"

Jordan shrugged. "I've seen things. Besides, most of 'my kind,' as you say, think I'm stupid for not wanting to drink blood directly from people."

"Aren't there other vampires who think like you?" Noah asked, curious. "Pacifistic ones?"

"Maybe." Jordan didn't sound convinced. "I've never met any before."

I'm sure they must be out there. But Noah knew how he felt. It was like when his sister or aunt tried to tell him, *There are still kind, accepting people in the world*, but after enough negative social interactions, Noah just didn't have the energy to keep looking for them anymore. He was hurt and jaded enough that he'd decided it was better to be alone.

"So...truce?" Noah offered. "I won't shoot you in the head if you don't drink my blood?"

Jordan started. "I...sure. I wouldn't...you know."

"What was all that talk about killing me in my sleep, then?"

"I *wouldn't*, but I *could*," said Jordan as he returned his gaze to the ground. "I'm a vampire. I'm a monster by nature."

Not that Noah had had the chance to chat with a vampire before, but Jordan was definitely the most self-hating vampire he'd ever met. Then again, he couldn't help wondering if, even after eight decades, Jordan was still somewhat traumatized by having been turned into a vampire without his consent. It seemed like something that someone wouldn't easily get over.

The doorbell rang, startling Noah from his thoughts. Wondering who it was, he went to open the door.

His sister, Elsie, stood in the doorway, her eyes bright. Noah gulped.

"If you ever try that again, I will *kill* you," she said.

"Um...sorry?"

She nearly crushed his ribs with a fierce hug. Noah bore it for as long as he could before he grunted, and she let go of him, stepping back.

"I *am* sorry," he said softly. "I didn't mean to make you worry."

She crossed her arms and pursed her lips. "Which was why you didn't tell me you'd volunteered for an elite hunt?"

He winced. "I just...I wanted the experience. And it was the first time a hunter had died in years. I didn't think..."

Elsie blew out a sigh. "Noah, do you *have* to do this job?"

Here we go again. They'd had a bitter argument—considering they rarely seriously argued with each other—when Noah first joined as a hunter. Since then, Elsie never tried to force him to quit, but she *did* try to change his mind once in a while. Or at least move back to Investigations.

"It's hard to find a job that I can do and that will hire me, considering my qualifications in this job market," Noah said, practically reciting the words from memory. "If I find a different job I can do *and* get a job offer, then

I'll consider it. Until then, I need to pay the rent somehow."

Elsie sighed again and walked into his kitchen. She started. "Who are you?"

Oh. Whoops. He should've warned her about Jordan, who was standing against the cabinets with his shoulders hunched, as though he wanted to disappear into the wall.

Noah cleared his throat. "Elsie, Jordan. Jordan, this is my sister, Elsie."

Jordan ducked his head a little. "How d'you do?"

"Nice to meet you." Elsie glanced between the two of them, her eyebrows rising. Noah had no idea how to explain without freaking her out with the exact details of what had happened, but he knew she wouldn't leave him alone until he told her something about who Jordan was.

"Jordan's my...friend," Noah said. Was he? He supposed, given that Jordan saved his life, they counted as friends...probably.

"Friend," Elsie echoed. "A new friend, huh?"

Noah frowned at her tone. "He's my *friend*," he repeated, with emphasis, to make sure Elsie didn't get the wrong idea.

Elsie held up her hands. "Okay, okay. Well, maybe we could all get together for lunch or dinner some time?" She gave Noah a long look. Unlike some allistics, Elsie made good on her promises of getting together for a meal.

"Yeah, sure." Noah turned to Jordan and waited.

"Oh, um...sure?" Jordan sounded confused. That reminded Noah that he wasn't sure what Elsie would think if he told her Jordan was a vampire...but that was a problem he could put off until later.

"Great. You can tell me how you guys met and exactly what happened during the two weeks you were...away."

Now she was *definitely* giving Noah the death glare. Noah cleared his throat and let his gaze drift to the window as he shuffled a few inches away from her. "Yeah, sure," he said in a false casual tone. "Just as long as you promise not to flip out."

Elsie let out a long sigh. "You should call Aunt Crystal, you know. Never mind—I'll tell her to call you. She probably wants to hear from you in person."

"Uh-huh." Now Noah felt even worse. Their aunt—who'd stood in for their parents after they'd died—hardly got worked up about anything, yet he'd made her worry.

Elsie held her arms out. "Hug?"

Noah stepped forward and gave her an obliging squeeze, hoping it would ease her worries.

"I've got to get to work," she said, "but I'll see you this weekend, yeah?"

"Yeah, sure. Go save the world."

She snorted a little, brushing some locks of hair from his forehead. "I will. Nice meeting you, Jordan," she called, over Noah's shoulder.

"Nice meeting you," Jordan called back before Elsie waved at them and let herself out.

"So," Jordan said after the door closed behind her. "Your sister, huh?"

"Yeah."

"She seems nice." Jordan kept looking at the door, where Elsie had left. "I...had a sister, too," he said, his voice very quiet. After a long pause, he added, even more quietly, "I miss her."

Noah stared at him. He knew how devastating it could be to lose family, and his heart ached in his chest at the obvious pain in Jordan's words.

"I'm sorry," he said, feeling how inadequate his words were, but not knowing what else he could say.

"Thanks," said Jordan, his voice scratchy. Then, he cleared his throat and shrugged. "It was a long time ago."

Noah was pretty sure Jordan was just saying that to cover up his grief. As though pretending it didn't exist could create a shield from the pain and prevent it from hurting. He would know; it was the same tactic he'd used himself, many times before.

Benched at a desk job for the next month, with regularly scheduled psychiatrist meetings, was about what Noah expected after he'd reported in to Rob. Not that he minded. He'd had enough excitement for a long time...and enough nightmare fodder, too.

Meanwhile, Jordan hung around his apartment, leaving only to pick up blood pills once a week. He'd gone back to being quiet and withdrawn, and Noah found himself worrying about him. He began to wonder if Jordan had sustained emotional trauma—whether from his clearly unhealthy prior relationship, or from killing his partner of over seven decades.

The problem was that Noah was not only not a licensed therapist, but he was also supremely terrible at making other people feel better. His intuitive approach was to ask people why they were upset, but in the past, he'd accidentally angered people who thought either he was being nosy, or he should've already "known" why they were upset (by...reading their minds? He'd never understood that logic). Sometimes they got angry at the idea that he thought they *wanted* to talk at all, which made even less sense to him, because even with blah blah manly stoicism or whatever, how was he supposed to help if he didn't even know exactly how they were feeling? So then he tried to leave people alone, but that didn't really work either, because then they thought he just didn't care about their problems.

Basically, he sucked at dealing with people, and water was wet.

But the part that hurt him most was when people took his lack of social intuition as proof that he didn't care about them, or he lacked empathy. He *did* care, and he had so much empathy that sometimes he actually wished he didn't have it because it hurt so fucking much, but he just couldn't seem to broadcast his feelings on his face or translate them into a form that other people could understand.

When Noah was upset, he sought out distractions, and he wondered if Jordan was the same. He coaxed him into watching movies with him at night, starting with *The Dark Knight*, and Jordan did seem to cheer up a little bit, but not entirely. Finally, Noah decided to bite the bullet. "Are you okay?" he asked Jordan one day.

Jordan raised his head to look at Noah from where he was lying on the couch. "Yes, I...I'm fine. Why?"

Those words told Noah nothing about how Jordan felt. "You've been kind of quiet, that's all."

"Oh." Jordan's shoulders hunched. "Sorry."

"You don't have to apologize," said Noah, bewildered. "I just...hope you're doing okay after, uh..." He swallowed, mind racing to find a non-blunt way to put it. "After what happened to Julius."

Jordan blinked. "Oh," he said again and paused. Then, "I didn't mean to make you worry."

Noah felt like he was walking through a verbal minefield. "I mean...you've known him for...a really long time. It's okay to, uh...to grieve," he finished, hoping he didn't sound too stilted.

Jordan's mouth twisted. "Even though he killed your friends? And he would've killed you, too?"

"They weren't really my friends." It took Noah a moment to realize that his attempt to comfort Jordan made him sound like a callous douchebag instead. He rubbed his forehead, sighing. "Look...I'm not saying he *wasn't* a bad guy. And I'm obviously really thankful that you saved my life. But that doesn't change the fact that it must've been hard for you to...do what you did."

Jordan stared at his knees.

"I just...he did so many awful things," he murmured. "But for so long, I still wanted to believe he wasn't a bad person deep down, and that no matter what he did to me, he still...still loved me." His voice caught, and he leaned his forehead against his palm. "That sounds so *stupid*, doesn't it? And it makes me think that—that maybe I'm just as bad as he was."

"That is *not* true," Noah vehemently replied. "For God's sake, Jordan, you met him when you were only *nineteen*. And, okay, I don't know your full history with him, but from some of the things you've said—it's not your fault if he took advantage of your inexperience and your desperation to be accepted and loved."

Jordan's expression seemed to collapse on itself, and Noah silently panicked. *Shit, I fucked up again.* "I mean...uh..."

He didn't know what he meant, and he didn't want to dig himself into a bigger hole than he already had.

"Sorry," Noah mumbled and all but fled from the room.

The next day, Noah found himself typing *vampire psychology* into Google at work.

His excuse to himself was that he'd finished reviewing his stack of paperwork early and, not wanting to ask for more right away, decided to take an internet break. He wasn't exactly sure what he was looking for, other than a vague sense that Jordan might benefit from some kind of therapy.

The rabbit hole of Google search results that Noah tumbled down turned out to be enlightening. Before, Noah's knowledge of vampires had been mostly limited to their physical capabilities—what danger they posed to humans and how they could be taken down. But apparently there were academics out there who had been studying the psychological effects of near-immortality and the transformation into a vampire.

One passage caught his attention in particular:

> *According to the surveyed vampires, children cannot be turned into vampires; they die if the attempt is made. The youngest age at which it is possible to be turned into a vampire without significant risk of death is reported to be around seventeen, but such vampires appear to be rare. Elder vampires suggest that humans who are turned into vampires at younger ages tend to suffer from emotional instability as time goes on. Reasons for such emotional instability could include greater trauma from the transformation process and inability to reach physical maturity.*

That did not sound promising. Noah was pretty sure the fact that Jordan had never consented to become a vampire hadn't helped matters.

Noah tried to search for something like vampire support groups, but he didn't turn up anything. Though, upon reflection, he realized that maybe if groups like that existed, they wouldn't want to advertise on the internet, just in case anti-vampire humans showed up.

Noah was not the biggest fan of asking people for information in person, but it beat making a phone call, so before he headed home for the day, he stopped by the blood bank again.

"Hi," he said to the receptionist. He cleared his throat. "Um...I had a quick question. I...have a friend who's struggling with, uh...vampire stuff. Like, psychologically. Are there any resources that I could pass on to him?"

The receptionist nodded, reached for something on her desk, and passed him what looked like a brochure. "There are some support groups in the area. That brochure has some information."

"Oh." *Sweet.* That was exactly what he'd been searching for. "Thank you so much."

He headed home, trying to think of the most casual, unobtrusive way to bring the subject up to Jordan.

"What do you think about attending a support group?" Noah asked.

Jordan frowned at him over the mug of water he'd dissolved his blood pill in. "A...what?"

Noah's definition of "casual and unobtrusive" meant initially trying to introduce the topic through a convoluted metaphor that only succeeded in confusing the hell out of them both. Finally, he lost his patience and just decided to ask directly.

"It's like…a group for people who have something in common—alcoholism, drug addiction, an illness—to support and help one another cope with what they're all going through."

"Oh." Jordan was frowning slightly. "And you think I should join a…support group? Why?"

Noah brought out the brochure he'd gotten earlier. "They have a group out in Lexington called 'Vampire Survivors of Violence'—for people who have been turned against their will, and people who struggle with being a vampire generally."

Jordan glanced away. "That's…nice, I guess, but I was turned almost eighty years ago. I'm not sure it's really relevant to me."

Noah was stuck. He knew, based on personal experience, that people couldn't be forced into therapy or self-help, but he *also* knew that internalized ableism was a barrier to getting help for many people. Especially, he assumed, for someone who grew up in the 1930s.

The problem was how to persuade Jordan in a way that wasn't pushy when Noah had almost zero persuasion skills.

"I'm sure they wouldn't, like, kick you out for being too old," Noah tried.

Jordan's fingers twitched around his cup, and he blinked a few times. *Oh. Bad move?* Noah wracked his mind for another route to take.

"I'm not an expert or anything," Noah said awkwardly, "but it seems like you've…been through a lot. And it might help to…talk to people who might've been through something similar. Or not even talk, if you don't want to, but just listen…"

He wasn't selling this very well, judging by Jordan's lack of reaction. He thought harder.

"I...well..." Noah swallowed. "I had a hard time when my parents died and then again in college, and...therapy helped me."

Jordan didn't respond to that, though his fingers tightened around his mug.

"And," Noah continued, "I know we live in a messed-up system where you can't access therapy without money, but something like a support group...could help. At least, it couldn't hurt. And I mean, I don't know what attitudes about mental health were like during your time, or whether you bought into the idea that people, especially men, can't talk about their feelings, or whatever. I know what it's like to feel awkward and scared asking for help, believe me. But...it's not worth suffering alone," he finished in a near whisper. "It's really not."

Jordan still didn't respond. Finally, after a long moment of silence, he sighed, his shoulders sagging.

"Okay," he said in a quiet voice. "I'll go. Or...try? I..." He bit his lower lip, staring down into his mug.

Noah began to feel a bit guilty. "It's your choice, obviously. I'm not trying to force you to go."

Jordan pushed out a breath. "I just...I...I don't know if I *can*."

Noah sat there, trying to understand what Jordan was saying. "If you really don't want to, you don't have to," he repeated. "Or I could...come along. For moral support."

Jordan looked up at him. "You...would?"

"Um...yeah. If you wanted me to."

Jordan lowered his gaze again. "If...it's not too much trouble. I'm sorry for being a bother."

"It's fine," Noah said, hoping his voice sounded reassuring. "Don't worry about it. Really."

So Noah drove Jordan to the location of the VSV meeting that evening. He wasn't as anxious as he would've been if he'd been walking into a social interaction with high stakes, but he was still nervous about going somewhere he'd never been, meeting strangers, and not having that much of a sense of how the meeting was going to go ahead of time.

The address on the brochure brought them to a nice two-story colonial house. Noah killed the engine and glanced at Jordan in the passenger seat, staring at his hands. He guessed he wasn't the only one feeling nervous.

"Ready?" he asked.

Jordan exhaled and nodded.

The front door was unlocked, so they let themselves in and followed the low sound of voices to what appeared to be the living room, with a circle of chairs arranged in the middle. As soon as Noah entered the room, he felt everyone else's eyes turn to him, and he took a step back. *Oh, fuck.* The fact that vampires could distinguish humans by smell had somehow completely slipped his mind.

Jordan stepped in front of him. To...shield him from view? "This is my friend," Jordan said. "Can he stay here?"

"I can go," Noah said, quietly.

Jordan turned to him, eyes wide. But before he could say anything, one of the other vampires—a bronze-skinned woman with dark hair—spoke.

"Of course you can stay. Forgive us; we're not used to having humans at these meetings. But, by all means, you're welcome to stay with your friend."

"Thanks," Noah said, relieved. He took a seat next to Jordan.

The group numbered about a dozen vampires, and they went around and did introductions—probably for Jordan and Noah's benefit. The vampire who first spoke to them, who introduced herself as Alex, opened the conversation by asking if anyone had something they wanted to share.

A vampire with a shock of dyed hair and multiple piercings raised her hand. Her name was Laura, Noah remembered, and she began talking about how she saw a stain on the sidewalk the other day, and somehow it reminded her of a time when her roommate had been attacked by her vampire ex, and she felt guilty for not having been able to protect her.

"It felt like a kind of flashback," Laura said, twisting one of the rings around her fingers. "All week I was feeling shitty about myself because it was my fault that she was attacked."

"Past regrets are difficult to let go of," Alex commented. "The fact that we live so long can make it harder, not easier, to let go of such feelings. I have to make a point to affirm to myself that the past is in the past, and no matter how much I regret it, there's nothing I can do to change what happened, so I have to let it go. Does anyone have ideas for coping strategies?"

The conversation that followed was a mix of suggestions and other people sharing their experiences. Some of the things they mentioned were familiar to Noah; they reminded him of what his various therapists had told him in helping him deal with his grief over the loss of his parents. He listened with intent curiosity, though as time passed, his energy began to flag. Thanks to his hyper-empathy, he got easily depressed by sad stories, which was why he usually avoided the news like the plague.

Near the end of the hour, Jordan raised his hand. The movement was tentative, hesitant, as though he wasn't sure whether he wanted to speak or not.

"Jordan?" Alex gave him an encouraging smile. "Is there something you wanted to share?"

"I..." Jordan let his hands fall to his lap and stared down at them intently. There was a long silence—the kind of silence that would've made Noah anxious, but everyone in the room just seemed to wait patiently before Jordan finally continued. "A long time ago, I...met...someone. Someone who I..." He swallowed hard. "Who I thought I could trust."

It wasn't hard for Noah to fill in the blank: *Julius Saint Laurent.*

"Then he turned me while I was asleep. Obviously, I shouldn't have trusted him." Bitterness seeped into Jordan's voice. "But I still did. I don't know. I was only nineteen, and I didn't have anyone else. I forgave him, but I...I told him I didn't want to drain people for blood, I *couldn't*, and I thought...I thought he would leave me be, and it would be okay. Then, one day..."

Jordan's voice faltered. After a moment of silence, he went on.

"One day, he brought a woman home. No—she was practically still a girl. He locked us in a room, together, and he said he wouldn't let me out until I...until I stopped denying what I was."

Noah's stomach knotted. Clearly, this story didn't end well. Jordan was curling in on himself, speaking to his lap.

"I begged him to let me out," he whispered. "I broke my shoulder trying to knock the door down. But in the end..."

He didn't finish. He didn't need to. The woman sitting next to him had put her hand on his shoulder, and he barely seemed to notice.

"The worst part was, that wasn't the only time," Jordan mumbled. "He would give up for a while, and then try again. And again. And again..." He seemed to crack, burying his face in his hands. "I wish he'd k-killed me instead," he sobbed out.

Noah's throat throbbed; he couldn't speak. Jordan's obvious pain was infecting him, and it was all he could do to keep a hold of himself and not weep in empathetic anguish.

"It wasn't your fault," the woman next to Jordan, the one who was patting his shoulder, murmured to him, as she passed him a box of tissues.

Others chimed in with comforting words until Jordan calmed down a bit. Soon after, the meeting ended, with Alex thanking everyone for attending and reminding them that there would be another meeting next week.

Jordan was completely silent on the way back. Noah was pretty emotionally wrung out himself, so he didn't think much of it until they got back to his apartment and Noah heard a whisper from behind him.

"Are you sure you still want me here?"

Noah turned around. Jordan's red-rimmed eyes were round, his hazel irises startlingly dark against the paleness of his face.

Noah cleared his throat. "I told you I didn't mind you being here, didn't I?" he said.

"Yeah, but..." Jordan didn't finish his sentence. Noah was usually the first one to break staring contests, but this time Jordan was the one who let his gaze flutter to the ground.

Noah stood there, awkwardly, not knowing what else to say. "Well, um...good night, I guess," he finally said.

"Good night," Jordan mumbled back.

Only a few days later did it occur to Noah to wonder about the fact that Jordan had introduced him as his friend. Did he really think of Noah as a friend, or was he just using "friend" as a shorthand, because "person who I've spent some time around and asked to come with me because I didn't want to be alone in a room full of strangers" was too long?

Eventually, Noah concluded that he was probably overthinking things, as usual. Most allistics had the habit of saying words that they didn't mean literally, anyway, so it wasn't worth obsessing over.

Chapter Eleven

Noah stood in front of the unfamiliar apartment building, feeling like a man walking to the gallows.

He'd thought he was done with interviewing strangers after he switched out from Investigations, but apparently not. Somehow, he'd forgotten just how much he'd disliked this part of his old job until now, when he had to do it again. He was beginning to regret not having a coworker he could pawn this part of his job off to.

After double-checking on his phone to make sure he was at the right place, he entered the building and pressed the buzzer for the apartment he was looking for. A female voice crackled over the intercom. "Who is this?"

Noah cleared his throat. "My name is Noah Lau; I'm with the VHA. I'd like to ask you a few questions about Tamara Johns."

The door buzzed as it unlocked, and Noah stepped through and headed up the stairs to the third floor. The woman who greeted him at her apartment door, Penelope Johns, was middle-aged, with dark, curly hair that spilled over her shoulders.

After they'd gone through the greetings and sat down at the kitchen table, and Noah had declined anything to drink, she asked, "Since you're from the VHA, does that mean Tam was...killed by a vampire?"

Noah frowned. That was not what he'd expected she would ask. "Um...yes. You weren't notified by a VHA investigator?"

She shook her head. "No. You're the first time anyone's come to tell me she's been found. Where...where did you find her?"

Somewhere in the back of his mind, Noah was starting to panic. Already, this conversation had gone completely off the rails from what he'd prepared for. "Uh...I'm sorry, Ms. Johns, but an investigator should've informed you about all of this...a few months ago. I'm just here because we've found some irregularities in our paperwork, so I wanted to verify some information. Are you saying you've never had contact with the VHA before?"

"No," she said, slowly. "I didn't even know for sure that she was dead until you showed up and I thought..."

Noah sat there, not knowing what to do or say next. All of the questions he'd meant to ask had been thrown out the window at this point.

"Um...well...in that case...thank you for your time, and I'm sorry to bother you," he said, awkwardly.

It wasn't until he'd left the apartment building that he'd realized he'd forgotten, in his confusion, to leave a card or ask her to contact the VHA if she remembered anything else, as was standard. *Oh, well.*

He took the T all over Boston to contact the other people on his list, growing more and more frustrated. *None* of the victims' next-of-kin that he managed to talk to had heard from the VHA before. Something was seriously wrong here.

Noah took an extended lunch break so he could remain blissfully conversation-free for an hour and try to regain some of his waning energy. He texted Jordan over his meal: *I'm already so done with today and there's still 4 hours left.* ☹

Jordan replied: ☺ *We'll relax tonight, ok?*

Noah smiled. *Ok*, he sent off, then sighed as he considered his next move.

He could continue to question the victims' families, or he could switch gears and question Darryl O'Brian. It was possible that he'd learn something new from one of the other victim's families, but he was rapidly losing faith in that line of questioning.

He made his way to Darryl O'Brien's bar in Fenway. When he went inside, he found it nearly deserted—not surprising, based on the hour.

"Excuse me," Noah said to the bartender, who was wiping the counter. "I'm looking for Mr. Darryl O'Brian?"

The bartender swiped her dyed red bangs from her eyes. "That's the owner. He only shows up at night, a few times a month."

"Oh." Noah frowned. If the owner rarely showed up at the bar, it seemed pretty unlikely that he'd witnessed multiple vampire attacks.

"Can I help you with something?" the bartender asked.

"Uh...I'm from the VHA," Noah explained, "and Mr. O'Brian's name is listed in connection with some vampire attacks. I just wanted to verify some information because there are some irregularities in our paperwork."

"Huh. I've never heard of anything as exciting as vampire attacks happening around here," she replied.

The queasy feeling in Noah's stomach that had started in the morning didn't get any better. "Have you worked here long?"

"About two years."

It was a long shot, but...Noah took out the reports from his bag and showed her the pictures of the vampires on them. "Do you recognize any of these people?"

"No, I...wait." She squinted and tapped one of the pictures. "He was a regular here, I think. And she looks kind of familiar..."

She didn't recognize all of the pictures, but she recognized enough that Noah was starting to be convinced that this wasn't a coincidence. "And you've never talked to the VHA? What about your coworkers?"

"Not sure about them. I only talked to a guy who comes by often and said he worked for the VHA."

Noah stopped dead. The queasiness in his stomach turned into full-on freefall.

"What did he look like?" he asked, the words coming out faint.

"A little less than six feet tall, strawberry-blond hair, blue eyes?"

That sounded unnervingly a lot like Casey O'Donnell.

"Hold on." He dug his phone out and scrolled through until he found a picture Jordan had taken of himself and Amy. He zoomed in until only the picture of Amy was visible. "Do you know this woman?"

The bartender studied the picture. "Oh, yeah. I remember her—she always orders a Bloody Mary when she comes. I haven't seen her in a while, though."

Noah thanked her for her time and wandered outside in a daze. He stood on the street, barely processing the noise.

Holy shit, was all he could think. *Holy* shit.

Noah had reached his "dealing with people" limit for the day, so he wrote up an email for Ariel that summarized his findings and sent it off before leaving work. His mind spun as he sat in rush hour traffic, going over what he'd learned.

The alleged victims in the tampered reports had not been confirmed dead by their family members.

Some of the vampires, including Amy, had frequented a bar that Casey O'Donnell had also suspiciously frequented.

The answer that could link all of these facts together, which was looking more and more plausible, was that Casey had somehow scoped out the vampires and made up some evidence, using publicly available names of missing persons, and then the VHA had sent hunters after them.

Casey couldn't have been working alone; he needed at least one person in Investigations to arrange the reports, and he probably also needed someone fairly high up in Investigations to sign off on everything, in spite of all the holes and shoddy evidence. So the question was, how many people were involved? And was Casey the ringleader, or only a henchman? He was pretty trigger-happy, but he didn't seem *that* anti-vampire...at least, not more than the average VHA employee. Maybe Noah was underestimating him, but he also didn't seem to Noah to be the kind of person who was...clever enough for this level of subterfuge. Then again, it wasn't like Noah could claim to understand him very well.

Noah felt sick. He didn't want to think that he'd been involved in taking out vampires that hadn't actually hurt any humans. But, perhaps more importantly, he had to tell Jordan what was going on right away. Casey had met Jordan; in the unlikely, but not impossible, event that he'd somehow managed to work out that Jordan was a vampire, then he was in danger of being targeted in the future.

Noah bounded up the stairs to his apartment two at a time, unlocked his front door, and stepped inside. The lights were on, but he didn't see Jordan right away.

"Jordan?" he called out.

No answer.

Weird, Noah thought. Jordan should have been back by now. Besides, both he and Jordan were in the habit of turning the lights off if they left the apartment. He texted Jordan on his phone: *Where are you?*

He set his stuff down and waited at the kitchen table for a minute. Two minutes. Five minutes.

Sure, sometimes Noah himself took way longer than five minutes to answer a text, but he was starting to worry. He tapped the icon to call Jordan in his contacts list.

Jordan's phone rang—in Noah's apartment.

Don't panic. Don't panic. Maybe Jordan just forgot his phone? Except Noah couldn't remember the last time Jordan had done that—he was typically glued to his phone just in case Noah had last-minute changes in plan due to his job.

Noah sat at the table, anxiety blossoming into full-blown fear.

Where the hell is he?

Chapter Twelve

FIVE MONTHS EARLIER

Noah usually disliked having roommates, but he didn't particularly mind having Jordan around. He was quiet and very neat (especially since he didn't need to eat anything other than blood pills); in other words, a fantastic roommate.

Jordan also had the alarming habit of tidying up around Noah's apartment, which Noah only realized after he'd come home from work a few times and found that the dishes and bowls he'd tossed into the sink in the morning had been magically washed, dried, and put away. Once, Jordan had even taken Noah's laundry up after Noah forgot about it, which embarrassed him.

"You don't have to...feel like you have to do my chores for me, as a way of paying me back or whatever," Noah tried to tell him, awkwardly. "I'm terrible at being an adult, but, seriously...you don't have to do this."

"I don't mind," Jordan demurred. "I'm used to doing these kinds of things. It's not a big deal."

That made Noah stop and blink at him. "Did...Julius force you to do all the work around the house?"

"Not—not really. It wasn't like that," Jordan said hurriedly.

Noah wasn't really convinced, but he decided to let the matter drop. Sure, he was more terrible than the average person at doing chores, but he didn't believe Jordan was doing all of this because he genuinely loved washing dishes and doing laundry.

Almost two weeks after Noah settled into his new routine of only reviewing paperwork, Rob texted him with an invitation to lunch. Normally, Noah wasn't a fan of spontaneous plans, but it wasn't like he had other urgent plans for lunch (besides enjoying some time by himself, which counted as a plan, dammit), so he met Rob outside the building and they walked to the nearby cozy Italian café Rob liked. They ordered and brought their lunches— arugula salad for Rob, mozzarella and pesto panini for Noah—to a quiet corner table.

"I've wanted to check in with you for some time," Rob said. "I'm sorry it's taken so long. It's been a bit hectic dealing with, you know, the aftermath of what happened to Gamma Squad..."

"Right," said Noah awkwardly. He didn't want to seem uncaring, but he still sucked at knowing how to react in these kinds of situations. He hadn't been kidding with Jordan when he'd said he barely knew them...or maybe being that close to death had caused his brain to shut down and compartmentalize. He chewed on his panini for a moment before coming up with something that was probably suitable to say. "It's very tragic."

He wasn't sure his vocal inflection was right, but Rob seemed to take it in stride. "Yeah. Seven skilled hunters, just...gone, in the blink of an eye. And you've been through a lot, too."

"I guess so," said Noah when Rob paused long enough to make it seem like he was waiting for a response.

Rob met his gaze briefly over the table. "How have you been, Noah? Really?"

"I've been okay." It was one of those scripted platitudes Noah had used so often that he practically said it without thinking, but it also happened to be more or less true in this case. As he'd told the VHA psychiatrist he'd been assigned to, he was sleeping okay, aside from the usual infrequent nightmare, and he wasn't feeling more anxious than usual or having any flashbacks to what happened.

Why his brain was better at dealing with a literal life-or-death horror situation than with the times when he'd messed up in a conversation was a mystery he'd probably never solve.

There was a pause before Rob went on, "I know...it must've been a horrifying experience, and I want you to know I'm here for you, Noah."

"Thanks," said Noah, since that seemed like what he should say. "I appreciate that."

More silence. He felt like Rob was waiting for him to say something, but he wasn't sure what. It wasn't that he didn't want to talk to Rob, but even though he'd known him for a long time, he still looked up to Rob with a bit of awe that made him try to tamp down on the urge to overshare about his feelings.

Rob cleared his throat. "I'm glad that you're okay. Being held captive by a vampire for two weeks...I was afraid of what that depraved monster might've done to you."

Noah shifted in his chair. "I'm lucky, I guess."

Rob sighed. "I've always felt responsible for you, Noah, after your parents—my friends—passed away. They were brilliant, you know. The world was robbed of the scientific breakthroughs I know they would've made."

Noah had known full well the importance of their chosen career. His parents had been scientists—a virologist and a physiologist—who both decided to switch to studying the vampirism virus and its effects. It wasn't just a critical public health issue; it was also a new Holy Grail in science. Many people believed that unlocking the secrets of the vampirism virus could lead to figuring out how to extend human lifespans and improved healing from currently lethal wounds.

"I wasn't the VHA director back then, but I felt like I'd failed them. And when your squad dropped off the map...I thought I'd failed them again."

"But you didn't," said Noah.

"I believed I did. I almost did. If something happened to you, especially because of vampires...I'd never forgive myself."

Noah set his panini down. "Are you suggesting I should quit?"

Elsie had argued with him bitterly enough, but Noah had never thought Rob had had any second thoughts about it.

Rob watched him. "Remember how I'd asked you why you wanted to work for the VHA?"

Noah nodded.

"And remember what you said?"

"Of course." His answer had been that he didn't want any other child to lose their parents the way he had.

"I can't stop anyone who has that kind of conviction from doing what they think is right." Rob's gaze turned distant. "Of course, that doesn't mean it's not difficult to bear the loss of hunters on my watch. It just reminds me that we're not doing enough—that *I'm* not doing enough—to protect humanity from vampires."

"You're doing the best you can," said Noah awkwardly. "We're all doing the best we can. Overall, the VHA is doing pretty well..."

"But there are still people who fall through the cracks," said Rob, sighing. "Still children who lose parents, and parents who lose children. I know I can't guarantee anyone's safety, but I'll do my damnedest to make sure what happened to Gamma Squad will never happen again." He met Noah's gaze. "Especially not to you."

"Thanks," said Noah, his voice rough with sudden gratitude.

Rob gave him a little smile. "You're one of the bravest people I know, though. After what you've been through, I wouldn't blame you if you said you never wanted to see a vampire ever again."

Noah chuckled...awkwardly. *Uh...right. And now I have a vampire roommate. No big deal or anything.*

There were moments when it struck him as odd, how completely his life had been turned on its head. And yet...in a way, it was even weirder that he spent most of his time *not* thinking about that.

"Um, thanks. Though I still think being a hunter is easier than talking to allistic people."

Rob arched a brow. "You're doing okay with me, aren't you?"

"That's different! I've known you, like, forever..."

And Noah was once again distracted from thinking about how his life had taken an unexpected turn by one of his favorite debate topics: whether there were logical rules to allistic conversations, or whether they just made no damn sense.

The only thing Noah got anxious about around Jordan was that he was terrible at making small talk; if forced to come up with topics for conversation, he tended to ramble about his special interests, which some people didn't appreciate.

"So...you really like Batman, huh?" Jordan asked once, after Noah had accidentally launched into a detailed monologue about the differences between the various film incarnations.

"Um...yeah," said Noah a bit nervously. He'd learned that usually, when people said something like that, it was their way of hinting to him to shut up.

"Because he also...lost his parents?"

"Well...yeah. We do have that in common." Noah shrugged, not looking at him. "When I felt down about my parents...it helped to remember Batman went through that, too. I mean, some people talk about how dressing up as a bat and beating up criminals probably isn't the best way to deal with trauma, but I liked thinking about how he was able to channel the grief and pain to do something good."

Jordan nodded. "That's a nice way to think about it."

Noah wasn't sure if Jordan was just being polite. Maybe he only listened to whatever Noah infodumped about because he was more than a little behind on pop culture. (Apparently Julius had been snooty and looked down on pop culture for being too "low brow." Also, he'd never given Jordan either a computer or a phone with access to the internet, which Noah thought was a crime in and of itself.) Jordan spent a lot of time reading Wikipedia and asking Noah all sorts of questions about pop culture and modern society, and Noah was quite happy to explain, even if he didn't always have the answers.

He got Jordan addicted to video games, which he wasn't at all sorry about. He also let Jordan borrow his phone to fiddle with his apps.

"What's Grindr?" Jordan asked one day as Noah was trying to make scrambled eggs.

Noah fumbled and dropped an egg. It landed in the sink and cracked, splattering. "Crap. Uh, well, it's an app for guys to date or hook up with other guys."

"It's...what?" Jordan said, in an odd voice.

Noah turned to look at him. "An app for guys to date or hook up with other guys," he repeated.

Jordan stared down at Noah's phone on the table. "I...wow. Really? I mean I know things are different now, but..." He raised his head to meet Noah's gaze, suddenly frowning. "You've...used it before?"

Noah rubbed the back of his neck. "Uhh...once or twice? My sister was the one who suggested that I get the app. It ended up not really being my thing, though."

Jordan was still staring at him. "But that means...you're queer? I mean...gay?"

Noah stared back at him. All this time, he'd forgotten that he'd never actually come out to Jordan. "Uh...yeah. Well, I don't identify as gay." He shifted on his feet. "I identify as pansexual—I'm attracted to people regardless of gender."

"Oh." Jordan's eyes were wide. "So...you've been attracted to men *and* women before?"

"Yeah."

It occurred to Noah that he wasn't sure exactly how...up to date Jordan's knowledge of the LGBTQ+ umbrella was. And it wasn't as though Noah had never experienced cis gay guys even in the twenty-first century heckling him simply because he had the *potential* to be attracted to women. He swallowed hard, watching Jordan's reaction anxiously.

Jordan looked at Noah's phone for a second longer before shifting his gaze away. "Sorry," he murmured. "I...shouldn't have asked such a personal question."

"Well," said Noah awkwardly, "it was probably obvious, since I had Grindr on my phone." He decided he should probably delete the app, though, since he didn't use it anymore. "I don't mind talking about it with you."

Jordan fidgeted in his seat and uttered an abrupt laugh. "Good grief...I never could've imagined such a thing being possible when I was growing up. Or that eventually, people could feel comfortable talking about being attracted to their gender." He sighed. "Heck...I grew up when it was only 'queer'—or worse words—and now there are so many different variations."

Noah decided to take Jordan's comment as positive. "Yeah, we're up to LGBTQIAP now," he said, "and there are people who don't like that because it's still not inclusive of all sexual orientations or gender identities."

"That's a mouthful," Jordan murmured. "'P' would be pansexual, right? What about 'Q,' 'I,' and 'A'?"

"'Q'—queer or questioning, usually. 'I' is for intersex, and 'A' is for asexual, aromantic, or agender."

Jordan frowned a little. "What are those?"

"'Agender' is someone who identifies as having no gender. 'Asexual' refers to someone who doesn't experience sexual attraction, or experiences it very rarely. It's kind of a spectrum. 'Aromantic' is similar—someone who doesn't experience romantic attraction or experiences it rarely."

Jordan was still frowning. "Um...could you repeat the definition for 'asexual'?"

"Asexual—no experience of sexual attraction, or it happens very rarely, in the case of gray-asexuals or demisexuals. Asexuals might still experience romantic attraction, or they could also be aromantic. Um...do you want me to give you some websites to look at?" Noah asked, feeling like he might not be explaining it very well.

"Y...yeah, that would be helpful," Jordan murmured.

Noah got his laptop, pulled up some asexual 101 resources, and handed it over to Jordan. As Jordan read, Noah cleaned up the cracked egg in the sink and stared at his remaining eggs in the carton before deciding, *Fuck it, scrambling eggs today is too much effort.* He put the eggs back into the fridge and pulled out a box of cereal instead.

Noah ate his cereal and surfed the internet on his phone for comic and other relevant news. When he'd nearly finished eating, however, he realized Jordan had his head in his hands and was no longer reading.

"Jordan?" Noah said, hesitantly. "Are you...okay?"

Jordan drew in a shaky breath through his fingers. "I...I thought I was broken," he whispered.

Noah's stomach dropped as he realized what Jordan was saying. *Oh. Shit.* He swallowed a mouthful of soggy cereal. "So...you think you're...? Um." He mentally kicked himself. "Not that you have to tell me anything, of course—just—uh."

Jordan dragged his hands over his face and then stared down at the table. He either didn't notice Noah's awkwardness or decided not to comment on it. "I think I'm...asexual. Gray-asexual, maybe? I thought it was just because of the way I was raised, at first," he began, in a slow, unsteady voice. "Because I grew up believing sodomy was a sin. But as the years went on, Julius grew impatient with me, and I...I wasn't so sure anymore...I didn't know what was wrong with me..."

That was a feeling Noah could relate to all too well.

"Well...if you want to talk about it with other aces, you could always join a forum," said Noah. "Other people could, like, help you figure stuff out and validate your experiences." It was something that had helped Noah out a lot when he was in high school and college, trying to make sense of being autistic in a world catered to allistics.

"Yeah," Jordan said softly. "I guess."

Maybe he was unused to the idea of chatting with people online, so Noah added, "Or you can just lurk on the forums. Read what other people write. I do that a lot."

"Mm." Jordan's fingers gently tapped on the table. "I was wondering...I guess a relationship between an asexual and a non-asexual would be hard, right? Or even...impossible?" he added in almost a whisper.

Noah couldn't help wondering if Jordan was talking about his relationship with Julius, and whether this was part of how their relationship had turned sour.

"I...don't want to say it's *never* difficult. But there *are* people who make it work. Some asexuals are okay with having sex to please their partner, some allosexuals— that's non-asexual—don't think sex is critical in a relationship...it can work."

"Is that what you think?" Jordan blurted out suddenly. "Would you date an asexual person?"

Noah blinked at him, more taken aback by the force and urgency in his tone than by the question. Jordan looked down at the table, two spots of color blooming on his cheeks.

"I...I'm sorry," he mumbled. "I shouldn't have asked...I'm sorry."

"Uh...that's okay, I don't mind." Noah cleared his throat. "I think I would, if, you know, we were otherwise compatible. I don't think I'd necessarily care if my partner wasn't sexually attracted to me. I, um..." He wondered, for a second, if what he was about to say was a bit TMI, but then he plowed on, "I like sex, and I like having sex in a relationship, but I definitely fall into the 'sex isn't the most important part of dating' camp."

"Oh." Jordan exhaled. "I see. Um...thanks for answering." He rubbed at his face, his cheeks still pink. "I know that was kind of...private."

"I don't mind," Noah repeated a little awkwardly. He didn't usually like talking about his sex life, but in the context of helping another person figure out their sexual orientation, he was okay with it.

Jordan didn't say anything else on the subject, so Noah stole a glance at his watch and excused himself to head off to work. He was nearing the end of his one-month period of being benched, and he was actually somewhat looking forward to returning to work as a hunter. Handling paperwork all day every day was deadly boring to him.

He made a beeline for the coffee machine in the break room as soon as he arrived—only to nearly have a heart attack on his way back.

"Yo, Lau!"

A forceful blow to Noah's back made him stagger forward, nearly spilling coffee all over himself. He clamped down *hard* on the urge to yell at the offender for almost knocking him over and turned to face the speaker.

It was Casey O'Donnell, one of the hunters from Delta Squad. From Noah's brief previous contacts with him, he'd seemed to be the kind of boisterously extroverted neurotypical person that Noah usually didn't have much luck connecting with.

"Hey," said Noah through his teeth.

Casey grinned at him, all blue eyes and strawberry-blond hair. "C'mon, you've got to tell us your tricks!"

"Tricks?" Noah echoed, his annoyance replaced by confusion.

"You know." Casey leaned in closer, making Noah inch back. "How you survived being held captive by that vampire for two weeks."

The suddenness of his question made Noah's mind go blank. He scrambled for some kind of acceptable answer. "I don't have any tricks. I just...got lucky."

"Aw, c'mon!" Casey laughed. "Luck? That's all you've got to explain how you outlasted Eddie Jesperson and two squads' worth of experienced hunters?"

Noah didn't know what to say, so he kept quiet. This was what he'd dreaded—being questioned about how he, the rookie, managed to be the only survivor out of a group of seasoned hunters. He was doing his best not to betray Jordan's existence, but he also wasn't great at maintaining complex lies.

Eventually, Casey shrugged. "Maybe I'll figure it out some day if you join us."

Joining Casey O'Donnell's squad? Noah wasn't sure if he was entirely looking forward to the idea.

"I used to be in Eddie's squad, you know," Casey added.

"Oh," Noah said awkwardly. Belatedly, he wondered if it was appropriate for him to offer condolences, but before he could decide, Casey was already speaking again.

"Damn shame to lose him." Casey sighed before straightening up and grinning at him again. "So? How's the promotion going?"

Noah frowned, baffled. *Promotion? What?* "I haven't been promoted. I'm just benched from taking any hunter assignments."

Casey looked at him. "I was joking."

"Oh." Heat flushed Noah's face, and he looked away, feeling utterly stupid. He normally prided himself on being able to distinguish sarcasm, but once in a while, he still slipped up. And it was always embarrassing.

"Right," Casey suddenly said. "You're not good at sarcasm, yeah?"

Noah's head jerked up. "How did you—" His mouth clamped shut as cold realization washed over him. "What—did Jespersen say something?"

"Uh...that you have autism?"

"That's *private* information," Noah hissed, all too aware of the fact that they were standing in an open hallway. Was there anyone nearby who'd overheard? He didn't want to have to deal with even more ableist assholes than he already did.

Casey blinked. "What? I mean, it's not like it's a secret, right?"

In a way, it kind of was. Noah had always suspected that one reason people almost never pegged him as autistic on sight—aside from the fact that most people had an abysmal understanding of what autism actually was— was due to his race. White people tended not to think it odd if an East Asian guy was quiet, socially withdrawn, and not big on eye contact. In any case, he preferred having complete control over deciding whether and who to tell about his being autistic. Because society was ableist and crappy, and he didn't have the time or the energy to fight against everyone's inaccurate preconceived notions, or explain why he wasn't like Rain Man for the gazillionth time.

"It's private, okay?" Noah repeated, trying not to snap. "Don't tell anyone else."

He left, fuming. He normally didn't like cursing out the dead, but seriously. *Screw Jespersen and his total lack of respect for other people's privacy.*

Around lunchtime, his temporary supervisor, Erin, tapped on the wall of his cubicle. "Hey, Noah. Everyone in the office is headed out for lunch at the Indian place across the street to have a farewell lunch for Nikita. Would you like to come along?"

Noah thought about it, but he'd brought lunch, and Indian food wasn't really his favorite. Besides, he wasn't even sure who Nikita was since he wasn't officially part of the administrative department, and he'd planned to use his lunch break to find more resources about asexuality for Jordan. "Thanks, but I have some things to take care of during lunch."

"Okay, well, can you cover the phone for the department until we come back?"

Noah froze. *What?* "But—I—I can't—"

"I know you're not officially part of this department, but we normally expect everyone to pitch in in terms of covering the phone, and you're the only one left to do it today. You can take your lunch break after we get back. Okay?"

In between trying to grapple with this abrupt change in plans, wondering whether he could take back his refusal and say "Just kidding, I don't have any plans after all and Indian food sounds really great right now," and also trying to figure out whether he should explain he couldn't take phone calls without extreme anxiety because he was autistic (which was totally in his employee file), Noah missed the window to respond, and Erin said, "Great! You can use my office. Thank you so much."

And she left him to wallow in misery and seething irritation.

Noah put his head down on his desk, focusing on the pressure between his forehead and the hard surface.

Look on the bright side, he tried to tell himself after he'd calmed down a bit. *It's lunch time for everyone. Maybe no one will call.*

He kept telling himself that right up until he'd settled behind Erin's desk and her phone started ringing.

By the time Noah left work, he was completely fried.

He'd taken longer than half an hour for his own lunch break because he didn't give a fuck anymore. (Also, if everyone else spent an hour at that Indian restaurant, why couldn't he get an hour for lunch, too?) It felt like every goddamn person decided to call the admin department at noon that day, for some reason, and he fumbled a bunch of the calls, tripping up his words and social scripts under the pressure of communicating to a disembodied voice, which only made him feel *more* anxious and embarrassed. He spent the rest of the day with his earbuds in, battling a headache, and not really having the energy to accomplish much else.

Scratch what he said before—he couldn't *wait* to return to being a hunter again.

When he got back, he found Jordan sitting at the kitchen table. Jordan glanced up and said something, but though Noah could hear him clearly, he had no idea what Jordan was saying.

"What?" he asked, his exhausted brain slowly sliding into panic mode.

Jordan's brow wrinkled. He spoke again, but the sounds still only registered as gibberish to Noah.

Aw, fuck. He normally didn't have auditory processing problems, but when he was extremely tired or distracted, his brain sometimes slowed down in terms of turning spoken language into meaning.

He covered his face with his hand. "Sorry...I'm really tired." He staggered over and collapsed onto the sofa.

He heard Jordan quietly pad over and crouch down next to him. More sounds that Noah's brain struggled to process. Jordan's voice was nice to listen to, though; soft and soothing, with that faint trace of a lilting drawl, and it didn't aggravate Noah's ragged nerves. In fact, he could've listened to it forever. This time, though, his brain only took a minute to figure out what Jordan had said—or part of it, at least.

"Anything I can do to help?"

Noah blinked. The question took him by surprise. He wasn't used to people asking him that.

"I just need to rest," he mumbled. Belatedly, he remembered to add, "Thanks, though."

Jordan left him alone, and Noah curled up on the sofa with his earbuds in, listening to his favorite songs on loop, the dull ache in his head ebbing and flowing like the tide.

Time passed in a haze before Noah was aware of someone tapping his shoulder. He started, nearly falling off the couch. "Mmphwhuh?"

"Sorry! I didn't mean to startle you." Jordan held his hands up. "I was just wondering...have you had dinner yet? It's kind of late."

Noah's stomach chose that exact moment to growl, adding to his embarrassment. It was considerate of Jordan to ask, but it also made Noah feel guilty. He shouldn't need other people to remind him to eat.

"I'll just...grab something from the fridge." He got up, with an effort, and wandered over to peer at what was inside his fridge. Milk, eggs, chicken broth...*Ah, damn it.* Chicken noodle soup sounded fantastic right now, but there was no way Noah had the executive function to cook.

Well, thank God for food delivery apps. Noah didn't know what he'd do if he had to order by phone. Starve for the night, he supposed.

He ordered food, ate, and crashed on the couch again. Hopefully Jordan wasn't expecting much scintillating conversation from him.

Noah didn't realize he'd fallen asleep until he became aware of someone carrying him, bridal-style, then laying him carefully on what felt like his bed.

Well, that's new, he managed to think as the blankets were gently tucked around him. His groggy mind realized, *Ohh, I fell asleep where Jordan normally sleeps. Whoops.*

He thought about how he hadn't showered yet, how he had to change into his pajamas, and how he should probably thank Jordan and apologize to him. Before those thoughts could translate into action, though, Jordan had closed the door to Noah's room softly, almost silently, and Noah's exhaustion dragged him back under.

Chapter Thirteen

Noah's thumb hovered over Ariel Cross's name on his phone. He'd been staring at her contact info for the past ten minutes, his heart thudding in his chest like a runaway rabbit.

His first, panicked instinct had been to call Elsie—his elder sister, his rock, the person he'd always looked up to any time he didn't know what to do. He had a feeling that he'd ended up babbling semicoherently, but Elsie seemed to get the gist.

"Maybe you could call the police?" she suggested.

He chewed on his lower lip. "Do the police handle missing vampire cases?"

The silence on the other end of the phone did not reassure him.

"Okay, well, how about someone at the VHA?"

"Els, the VHA is about *hunting* vampires, not tracking down missing ones..."

"You said you were working on a secret project for your squad leader when you found out about the possible rogue vampire killer or whatever, right? Why don't you contact her, explain the situation, and ask for advice?"

He instinctively resisted the suggestion. He'd been so careful to hide his relationship with Jordan from the VHA, and now...was he really going to go up to his squad leader and tell her about him, point blank?

Then again...he didn't know where else to go for help.

"Fine," he mumbled.

"Good luck," said Elsie in a serious tone. "Let me know what happens. I hope Jordan is okay."

"Thanks."

Gathering his courage, Noah finally texted: *Hi Ariel, I'm sorry to bother you, but I need help*, and he sent it before he could change his mind.

He waited for a reply. One minute crawled by. Then two.

He should've called, except Noah always hated calling people unless they were family. Listening to disembodied voices over the phone freaked him out because he was even worse than usual at deciphering tone if he didn't have any facial expression to go along with it. But what if Ariel was in the middle of something? What if her phone was dead, or she'd silenced it and wasn't going to check her messages until right before she went to sleep?

The sudden tone of an incoming text made him jump out of his seat.

Ariel: *No problem, what kind of help do you need?*

Noah was relieved at first, but then his anxiety came roaring back. Fuck, what was he supposed to say? *I think my boyfriend's gone missing, oh and by the way he's a vampire so it might be related to our investigation, maybe? Actually, who knows if it's related, but I didn't know who else to call for help?*

After a long moment of thinking, he texted, with shaking fingers: *I think someone might've come to my apartment because of what we've been looking into.*

Ariel quickly replied: *Are you at your apartment now? Are you ok?*

Yes. I'm ok, but... Noah hesitated longer, trying to find the right words. *I think I need help.*

Give me your address and I'll be right there.

Noah sent it off before he could change his mind. Then he was stuck waiting the long, agonizing minutes for Ariel to arrive. As usual, his mind scrambled to script the conversation in his head.

Hi Ariel, thanks for coming by on such short notice. I'm fine, but my boyfriend is missing. I think he might've been abducted because he's a vampire, and as I explained in my email, someone's been targeting vampires...

He was still in the middle of trying to polish his explanation when his doorbell rang, nearly giving him a heart attack. Swallowing hard, he went to answer it. Ariel stepped inside his apartment, looking as glamorous as always.

"Are you all right?" she asked again. "What happened, exactly?"

Noah's mouth went dry, his mind blanking. So much for trying to script his answer. "Um," he stammered, "I'm okay, but, uh...I came home, and the lights were on, but...my boyfriend isn't here. And he left his cell phone. I...I think someone might've...taken him away, somehow."

"Okay, um..." Ariel was frowning. "Not that I'm not worried about your boyfriend, but...if he doesn't work for the VHA, how can you be sure he's related to what we found?"

Noah fixed his eyes on the ground. This was it—the moment of truth.

"Well...he's...a vampire," he said in a very small voice.

A long moment of silence passed, during which Noah was painfully aware of the rapid beating of his heart against his ribcage.

"Oh," Ariel finally said.

Noah couldn't read her tone, and his anxiety worsened. What would she say next? *How did that happen?* or *How could you, a hunter, date a vampire?* or even *What's wrong with you?*

"Did anyone from the VHA know you were dating a vampire?" Ariel asked.

Noah sucked in a sharp breath, trying to grasp for words. "No...well, I was careful not to tell anyone, but this past week, Casey unexpectedly came by my apartment and met Jordan. He...he might've figured out he was a vampire, somehow..."

Although, how the hell did Casey ever become suspicious of him in the first place? Sure, Noah had been cagey in his answers about his personal life, but he didn't think it was *that* weird to say he wanted to keep his work and personal lives separate.

"Hmm." Ariel glanced around at his apartment. "You said you're sure your boyfriend—Jordan, was it?—made it home because the lights were on?"

"Yeah."

"And you didn't find any evidence of a struggle?"

Noah frowned. "No."

"If he'd met Casey before, then he probably would've opened the door for him, which explains that much."

"Makes sense," said Noah reluctantly.

Ariel folded her arms. "What I'm very curious about is why Jordan would've been abducted. It definitely wouldn't be easy for one human, or even a small team, to take a vampire in alive. And why him, in particular?"

Why him, indeed? Noah's stomach churned with unease.

"How old is he?" Ariel asked.

"Um...over ninety."

Ariel's eyebrows rose. "He must be pretty strong, then."

"I...I don't know. He's usually pacifistic." Noah hesitated before adding, "He did...kill a much older vampire before. Although that vampire was a little distracted at the time..."

"That *really* begs the question of how he could've been abducted without making a scene. And you live in an apartment building, so it's not like the kidnapper could've left with a body bag without drawing a lot of attention..." Ariel frowned. "Or perhaps he was verbally coerced into cooperating?"

Noah was starting to feel sick with anxiety. *Why him? Why him?* He couldn't think of an answer, and it was driving him out of his mind. "We have to tell Director Bellamy."

Ariel glanced at him. "Noah, I'm not sure if that's a good idea—"

"You're being careful, I know, but he's the branch director. He needs to know what's going on here. Besides, I've known him for years. We can trust him."

"But until we're sure we know everyone involved—"

"Jordan could be in danger!" Noah burst out. That was the terror slowly eating away at him: Casey or the rogue faction or whoever was to blame was out to kill all vampires, so whatever the reason they'd taken Jordan, it could not have been good. "I'm sorry, but I'm not going to wait until we have more information."

Ariel closed her mouth. "Okay," she finally said. "I'm not going to stop you. But just...be careful, all right?"

"I will."

He said goodbye to Ariel, grabbed his jacket and keys, and made his way to his car as he texted Rob, asking to meet. Rob would know what to do. He was the director; he *had* to know what to do.

Jordan's life may very well be depending on it.

Chapter Fourteen

FIVE MONTHS EARLIER

Gradually, Noah felt less awkward about showing up to the VSV meetings with Jordan, and he thought the others were getting used to his presence. At least, they seemed to smile at him more. Or so he thought.

At the end of one of the meetings, someone grabbed Jordan for a conversation, and Noah wandered off to get a drink of water. As he filled a little paper cup using the water dispenser, he couldn't help feeling uneasy.

He was glad Jordan was making friends, he really was, but there was also a part of him that couldn't help resenting how it was easier for Jordan than for him. Just as he loved his sister, but sometimes he resented, too, how she had so many friends and was always getting invited to this or that event on the weekends with them. It was the dark, not-so-nice part of him that he normally locked tightly away in the back of his mind and pretended wasn't there, but he couldn't help being aware of it when it surged to the surface once in a while.

"Hi. Noah, was it?"

Noah nearly dropped his cup as he spun around. One of the other attendees stood behind him, a pretty young white woman who appeared maybe Noah's age.

"Um, yes, hi," Noah stammered, his mind racing for her name. Was it Amy?

Amy smiled at him. "You're Jordan's friend, right?"

"Yeah."

"It's really cool that you're supporting Jordan through all of this. We rarely get humans showing up to be supportive."

"Yeah. Um, thanks," Noah said, momentarily confused. That *was* the right thing to say, since she'd sort of praised him, right? "Just...trying to be a good friend."

Amy tucked a lock of hair behind her ear. "So...do you work? Or study?"

"I...work."

"What do you do?"

Noah thought hard, trying not to panic. He couldn't very well say he was a hunter for the VHA, since that was a surefire way to get banned from the meetings for life. Then again, this *was* supposed to be a safe space, so he felt bad for lying. Fuck, he should've thought this through earlier.

The silence dragged. Amy was giving him a strange look. No doubt she was starting to think that his long pause meant he did something illegal for a living.

"I'm...a private security contractor," he blurted out.

"Oh." Amy nodded. "That's cool."

"Do you work?" he said hurriedly, trying to brush over the awkward patch in the conversation.

"Yeah. I'm a psychiatric nurse."

"Oh. Very cool."

The awkward silence came back, and Noah sipped his water nervously. He hated these moments in a conversation—the moments when he felt like he was supposed to know what to say next, but he didn't.

"Have you known Jordan for a long time?" Amy asked.

"Not really. I met him a few weeks ago."

"Ah. Fast friends, huh?"

Not wanting to get into the specifics of how they'd met, Noah answered, "Yeah, I guess so."

Unfortunately, he couldn't ask the same question back at her. He thought for a while until he came upon a question and grasped it with the relief of a man overboard clutching a lifesaver.

"Have you been coming to these meetings for a long time?"

"For the past few years," Amy replied. "I was lucky to have been referred here after...um, after my life changed. It's been very helpful. I've made some good friends here."

Noah nodded. "Yeah, I can imagine."

More awkward silence. More of Noah anxiously sipping his water for lack of something else to say, except the paper cup was tiny and he was running out of water. Should he refill it, even though he wasn't thirsty anymore? He tried not to turn away to glance at the clock. Was Jordan done talking yet?

Amy cleared her throat. "Well...it's kind of late. I should probably get going. I have a shift later tonight."

"Oh. Right." Noah tried not to sound too relieved.

"It was nice meeting you, Noah."

"Nice meeting you too. Good luck with your shift."

"Thank you," she said with one last smile and then left.

Noah let out a breath and chucked his paper cup in the trash. He turned around—and started as he realized Jordan had been standing behind him.

"Oh, jeez! Sorry. You startled me. Have you been waiting long?"

Jordan shook his head. "No, not at all. I was just waiting for you to finish."

Noah wondered how much of the conversation Jordan had heard, and he found his stomach twisting with embarrassment. Though...why should he be embarrassed? It wasn't like he was trying to impress Jordan with his nonexistent conversational skills or anything.

He thought Jordan had had a good time at the meeting, but Jordan slipped back into quiet mode on the way home. Maybe he was so horrified by Noah's inability to carry a conversation with other people that he was rethinking their whole friendship. Noah clutched the steering wheel tightly and tried to tell himself he was just being paranoid, but it wouldn't be the first time he'd had a friend—even a seemingly close friend—suddenly ghost him.

"How does one date in the twenty-first century?" Jordan asked the next morning, out of the blue.

Noah's mouthful of cereal got stuck in his throat. He swallowed hard, not sure why he suddenly felt so uneasy.

"Well...there are online sites or apps."

"Right, like Grindr." Jordan folded his hands on the kitchen table. "So people don't, like...meet in real life anymore?"

Noah choked on his cereal milk. "No—they do," he said, trying not to laugh. "It's just not always easy to find a good match from your immediate social circle. A lot of the time people go to bars or nightclubs to find a hookup or a potential date."

"Are there...those kinds of places here?"

"In Boston? Yeah. I mean, probably. I've never actually been to one." He wasn't social enough—or in need of casual hookups that badly—for that kind of excitement.

"Could we...go to one?" Jordan asked, sounding hesitant.

"Um...sure," Noah said, thrown. The request made him strangely apprehensive...but then again, Jordan had never asked for anything until now. If he wanted to party in the twenty-first century, Noah would be kind of a dick for saying no. He eyed Jordan. "Although...they might card you at the bar if they don't believe you're over twenty-one."

"Right..." Jordan sighed. "It's fine. I'm not a big fan of drinking, anyway."

Man, that's gotta suck, Noah thought. Being ninety-five years old but having no one believe Jordan was over the drinking age. Noah himself still got carded from time to time.

Jordan shifted in his chair. "I mean...I don't want to be a bother," he said softly. "If you don't want to go."

Noah waved a hand dismissively. "It's fine." He normally didn't go for loud environments, but how bad could it be?

It was bad.

Noah could hear the thrumming bass from outside the club, and loud dance music assaulted him as soon as they stepped inside. He could've sworn the bass was making his organs vibrate inside his body. How could people stand to listen to music at this volume without going deaf? The club was stiflingly hot, packed with sweaty bodies, and Noah could barely see in the dimness, punctured by erratic, flashing colored lights.

Jordan mouthed something at him, but Noah couldn't hear. "What?" he tried to yell over the music.

Jordan upped his volume, but Noah still couldn't make out the words. "*What?*"

"*This is really overwhelming!*" Jordan shouted.

At least he wasn't alone, then. Noah nodded fervently in agreement.

"*What do we do?*" Jordan asked.

Noah glanced across the sea of dancing bodies to the bar. The bar looked like an island of relative sanity to him, and already he desperately craved a drink. He pointed, and Jordan nodded, following him.

Noah ordered a scotch for himself and mineral water for Jordan (after the bartender gave Jordan a serious side-eye). As Noah drank, he watched Jordan, who gazed at the crowd between sips of water. Noah had lent him the closest thing he could find to "clubbing clothes" in his closet, which meant a dark-blue T-shirt a size too small for his taste, plus a pair of skinny jeans Elsie had bought for him that he didn't wear because the feel of denim rubbing right up on his skin was distracting to him. On Jordan, though, they looked good. He could've passed for a regular twenty-first-century teenager, out looking for a good time.

He wondered what Jordan thought of all this. His face had an unreadable expression. *I should've worn something flashier*, Noah found himself thinking and then, a second later, wondering why he'd even had that thought. *He* wasn't here to get laid. Besides, given how loud and crowded the club was, he was glad he'd at least dressed for comfort and worn his favorite red T-shirt.

Jordan opened his mouth, and Noah leaned in closer to listen.

"I feel really old," he said.

It would probably never *not* be surreal for Noah to hear that coming out of Jordan's mouth. That thought made him feel bad, though. Some of the things Jordan had said made it sound like he'd resented Julius for freezing him at the physical age of a nineteen-year-old forever.

"Well...you fit in pretty well," said Noah, gesturing. There were plenty of tweens, and possibly older teens, on the dance floor.

Jordan was still frowning. "You mean I *look* like I fit in, even though I'm the oldest person in this room."

Noah accidentally choked on his drink, the scotch burning his windpipe. *Yeah. Surreal.* Jordan had a point, though.

A laugh came from Jordan's other side at the bar. A muscular, well-built white guy who appeared to be in his thirties was watching Jordan over his drink. "Whoa there, kid. Some of us are actual adults, you know."

Jordan looked down, his fists clenching in his lap, a dull flush spreading across his cheeks. Noah wanted to defend him, but the suddenness of the stranger's comment took him aback and scrambled his ability to speak. Plus, he was pretty sure Jordan wouldn't appreciate being outed as a vampire in the club...

"Come on." Jordan jumped down from his stool and strode off into the crowd. Noah hurriedly downed the rest of his drink, paid his tab, and followed him.

Down on the dance floor, the music was even louder, the crush of dancing bodies making Noah flinch at every unexpected brush against him. Jordan glanced around at other people and started bobbing his body awkwardly to the music, and Noah bit down on his lip, trying not to laugh. It was...strangely endearing.

"I don't know what I'm doing," Jordan confessed. He leaned in close so Noah could hear, so close Noah could feel the puff of breath against his face. His skin prickled. It felt...too intimate, somehow.

"I don't think anyone does," Noah replied. Goodness knew he himself had no dancing skills whatsoever.

Jordan opened his mouth, but before he could speak, someone slipped between them—a guy who looked like a college student or fresh grad, albeit one who looked like he modeled in his free time. A tight T-shirt clung to his suntanned, leanly muscled frame, brown hair streaked with blond highlights flopped over his forehead, and the quartz studs in his ears glinted under the strobe lights as he threw Jordan a wide grin. "Hey."

Jordan blinked. "H-hi."

Noah watched the other guy lean toward Jordan, saying something into his ear that made Jordan laugh, and Noah's stomach twisted into nauseated knots.

It's not like I'm dating him.

Aside from the fact that Jordan had the "ninety years old but looks nineteen" thing going on, and a corpse-pale complexion, he *was* pretty, and when he wasn't brooding about his past history or angsting about being a vampire, he was caring and kind of sweet. Not like Noah, who tended to hover between social anxiety and a dour "fuck everything" attitude.

Noah suddenly felt claustrophobic in the crowd. He pushed his way out of it—past all the hot, sweaty bodies— and made a beeline for the bathroom. Which he almost regretted doing when he slipped inside and the stench of bodily fluids hit him in the face and nearly made him gag.

Noah splashed water on his face as he tried to breathe through his mouth. Even though it was quieter in the bathroom, he could still hear the heavy thud of the bass, coupled with the sounds of sex coming from one of the stalls, and he wished he'd brought noise-cancelling earphones to block it all out.

Fatigue washed over him as he leaned heavily over the sink, sinking into his bones and making his brain cells melt into mush. He was overstimulated. He wanted to go home. And he couldn't escape the confused feelings of jealousy that dogged him for reasons he didn't fully understand. He was afraid Jordan would ditch him for a new boyfriend. Or...was it more than that? The problem was he could hardly think between the noise and his exhaustion.

Even if Noah wanted to, he couldn't stay much longer without risking going into shutdown. He decided to tell Jordan he was going home.

As soon as he stepped out of the bathroom, the wall of loud dance music assaulted him again, and he cringed, finally giving in to the impulse to cover his ears. He tried searching for Jordan on the dance floor, but when he got to the spot on the dance floor where he'd left him, Jordan was nowhere to be seen.

Maybe he moved with the crowd.

"Jordan!" Noah tried to yell over the music, but even if Jordan had heard him, Noah wouldn't have been able to hear his reply.

Or maybe he found someone to go home with already. Wait, isn't he not into hookups? No...you don't necessarily know that. Maybe he found his true love at first sight.

Noah was approaching the limits of his tolerance, so he hastily made his way to the exit. When the door slammed shut behind him, he stood in the alleyway behind the club, breathing in the crisp, cool spring night, savoring the silence after having been bombarded with music in the club.

For a moment, he let himself indulge in a fantasy in which he had a boyfriend or girlfriend to hug him, soothing him with a deep pressure stim. He sighed.

"Noah?"

Noah jumped, his adrenaline spiking before he recognized Jordan's voice.

"Jordan! I-I was looking for you," he babbled, feeling both confused and relieved. "I thought you'd left. Um, with someone."

Jordan had his hands tucked in his jeans pockets. "I was looking for you too," he said softly. His brow wrinkled under the lamplight. "Are you okay? You don't...look so good."

"I don't?" Noah echoed. Usually, no one other than Elsie and his aunt could tell when he was overstimulated and in need of rest. He bit his lower lip, feeling a surge of...some unnamable feeling at Jordan's question. "I...I'm fine. Just tired," he murmured, too afraid to get into the details about autism. "I was going to go, but you can stay if you want."

Jordan shook his head. "No, that's okay."

Noah was about to tell him he didn't have to be so polite when he noticed Jordan's shoulders were slightly tense, his gaze lowered. "You didn't...have a good time?"

Jordan exhaled shakily. "I'm not...used to this," he said, his voice unsteady. "I *want* to be, but—I can't—"

Noah's stomach lurched. He'd thought Jordan was calm, but clearly he'd been way, way off.

"I'm sorry." Jordan cut himself off. "I know you're tired, and I don't mean to dump my problems on you. I'm sorry."

Noah didn't feel reassured. He *was* tired, but the only thing worse than that was Jordan being silently, utterly miserable.

"It's fine if it's not your scene, Jordan," Noah said a little awkwardly. "I'm not really...a fan of this environment either." *Though mostly because it's not autism-friendly*, he internally added.

"I thought I was okay with who I was," Jordan whispered. "You know...the gray-asexual thing. But I come here, and I feel wrong all over again."

Noah's throat tightened. "Don't say that. You're not *wrong*, Jordan—"

"I didn't fit in back then, and I still don't fit in now." Jordan shut his eyes.

"I don't fit in either," Noah said, the words rushing out of him. "I never have. And yeah, it sucks to feel like you don't belong, but..."

But...what? Saying things like "There are people who'll accept you somewhere out there in the world" or "You should embrace your difference anyway" sounded so cliché, so generic. They'd never helped Noah, so why would they help Jordan? And yet...what alternative did he really have? So much of social interaction seemed to revolve around reciting empty platitudes in order to show that you cared about other people.

"But...I'm sure...you'll find people who'll accept you some day," Noah stammered out, hoping he didn't sound too wooden. Maybe he should've offered Jordan a hug instead. Was that appropriate, or would it just be awkward?

Jordan huffed a flat-sounding laugh that made Noah's heart twist. "Yeah. Sure. My family is dead. The friends I used to have are dead, too. I killed my partner.

I'm a vampire, and apparently I'm not even the right kind of queer. Who's going to accept all of *that*?"

Noah's chest throbbed with a shared ache. *I know what that feels like*, he wanted to say. *You're not alone.*

An answer welled up in his throat, but he couldn't grasp the words he wanted. So Noah kissed him instead.

Jordan's lips were soft, pliant. When Noah drew back, he realized Jordan's eyes were wide and mouth open...in shock, probably. Possibly even in horror? Suddenly, he regretted his spur-of-the-moment decision. Fuck, what was wrong with him? He wasn't usually this impulsive.

"I'm sorry," he stammered. "I—"

Before he could finish, Jordan had wrapped his arms around Noah's neck and was kissing him back, sweetly yet desperately, as though he were afraid Noah would disappear.

"Oh gosh," Jordan gasped. "I didn't think you could— I didn't think—"

He uttered a sound that sounded suspiciously like a sob. "Jordan?" Noah said, beginning to panic.

"Sorry," Jordan mumbled, drawing back a little, his hands falling back to his sides. "I...I didn't think you could ever be interested in me. Because I'm a vampire, and...you're a vampire hunter. I...didn't know if I was *human* enough for you."

Noah instinctively bristled at the phrase "human enough." People had used similar phrases as a weapon against him before—claiming that autism somehow made him "less than human" because he "didn't have a theory of mind" or "couldn't love" or some bullshit like that.

"You *are* human enough," said Noah fiercely.

Jordan's eyes seemed to swim under the lamplight.

Not wanting to make him cry, Noah asked, "So...I'm not too young for you?"

Jordan stared at him before bursting into laughter. It was slightly hysterical sounding, but when he wiped his eyes, he was smiling.

"You're a little young," he said in a teasing tone that sent a thrill down Noah's spine. He'd never seen this...mischievous, *flirty* side of Jordan before. "But that's okay."

"Hey, not all of us can be ancient dinosaurs like you."

Jordan grinned. He glanced at Noah through his eyelashes, and *fuck*, every time he looked at Noah like that, Noah wanted to kiss him. He trailed his lips along Jordan's jaw, hearing Jordan's sharp intake of breath—

A sudden groan startled him, making him glance to the side to see two men pressed up against the brick wall and—*Ohhkay*. He wasn't squeamish about sex, but neither did he have any particular desire to watch two strangers getting busy with each other in an alley.

He glanced at Jordan, whose pale cheeks were flushed. "Uh...we should move," Jordan said.

"Agreed." He nuzzled Jordan's cheek. "Let's go home."

Sunlight against Noah's eyelids woke him up. He groaned and turned over, momentarily confused by sight of Jordan's bare back in his bed. Then he remembered.

Oh. Right. They'd had sex last night.

Jordan still seemed to be asleep, so Noah got up, dressed, and wandered over to the kitchen. He turned on the kettle, and after the water boiled, he sat at the table with a cup of jasmine tea, mulling over what had happened.

Ever since his last, very nasty breakup in college, Noah had sworn off dating. The truth was, he was tired of rejection and scared of experiencing it over and over again.

But he...liked Jordan. A lot. He'd missed having a companion or friend he could just talk to about anything without worrying about how weird he was coming off as, ever since Elsie had to move across town for her job. Jordan had filled that empty niche for him, and Noah was terrified that if they began a relationship and it went south, he'd lose not just a dating partner, but also a friend. And Noah was very, very short on friends.

His thoughts were interrupted when Jordan wandered in, stifling a yawn, his hair still rumpled from sleep. He was wearing Noah's pajama pants and oversized Batman T-shirt...and somehow, he'd never looked sexier.

"Hi," said Noah, his heart skipping a beat.

"Hi," Jordan returned with a soft smile that made Noah's insides melt.

It was the kind of smile Noah wanted to wake up to every morning, but...God, he'd been here before. Pinning his hopes on a romantic partner, only for it to all fall apart once they actually got to know him. Fuck the idea that "what doesn't kill you makes you stronger"; every previous rejection only knocked Noah down even harder than before, until he was scared of even trying anymore.

"What?" Jordan asked, his smile fading. "Is...something wrong?" He paused and then added, in a quiet, unsteady voice, "Was it that bad?"

"What—no!" Noah felt horrified that that was what Jordan assumed. "It was good."

Jordan let out a breath, but he still didn't smile again. "That's good. I..." His hands tightened on the hem of his borrowed T-shirt, and he swallowed. "Are you...really okay with...um, me being...asexual?"

Noah's heart throbbed in his throat at the thought that Jordan felt like he had to ask. "Of course I am."

"It's just..." Jordan spoke slowly at first, but then the words came out faster, in a rushed tumble. "I've been doing a lot of reading online, and—I don't know if I've understood it all yet, but—I think I experience sexual attraction sometimes, rarely, but I still have a low, uh, drive," he stammered, his pale cheeks reddening, "so...um...I just...don't want you to be disappointed..."

"Okay," said Noah.

Jordan blinked. "Okay?" he echoed. "That's...it?"

Noah shrugged a little. "I mentioned before that I don't think of sex as the most important part of a relationship, so...yeah. I don't think *that's* the thing that would be an issue."

Jordan's eyebrows knitted. "What do you mean?"

"I...I'm just..." He looked down and swallowed hard. "I'm scared of messing this up."

Jordan's bare feet whispered against the floor as he approached Noah. "How could you mess this up?" he asked, softly. "Unless you get a personality swap."

"No..." Noah bit his lip as he got up from the table and started pacing back and forth. "It's my current personality. Uh...not my personality, exactly. Maybe? I'm bad at relationships. I mean, not that I have problems with commitment or anything like that! That's not it at all. I'm fine with commitment. I...just..."

He was rambling, and if he hadn't scared Jordan off already, he'd probably just confused the hell out of him, and he had no idea how else to explain except to tell him the truth.

So many ways Noah had tried to deal with it...and so many ways it had blown up in his face. He'd tried hiding it—which only worked until Autistic Weirdness finally drove his exes away. He'd tried telling people upfront—which usually only scared them away faster. Or, in one memorable case, led to his then-partner insisting that he take social skills classes and therapy to sort of "fix" his autism. He'd tried not talking about it until he thought his partner would be receptive—which only resulted in his then-partner blaming him for "hiding" something so important, making him feel awful about himself. It was a lose-lose-lose situation.

"I'm autistic," he blurted out.

He watched Jordan's face anxiously, but he couldn't read his expression. Technically, he'd been diagnosed with Asperger's Syndrome, but now that the DSM-V had combined it into Autism Spectrum Disorder, he'd gotten used to thinking of himself as autistic.

"Oh" was all Jordan said, after a minute, in a similarly unreadable tone.

Noah let his eyes drift to the floor, going through all of the worst case responses in his head. *Thanks for the sex, bye now! I just remembered I had a friend who's willing to let me crash with them!* Or: *Why didn't you tell me earlier?* Or...

"So," said Jordan slowly, "what does that mean, exactly?"

Noah's head snapped up. "You've...never heard of autism before?"

"I've heard of it, but I was never exactly clear on what it was. I thought it was a mental disability." Jordan looked at him. "You don't seem...mentally disabled."

Noah sucked in a breath. He'd let that go, this one time, due to Jordan's lack of knowledge. Gosh, when was the last time he'd gone into autism infodump mode?

"Well, autism is a neurodevelopmental disability that encompasses a wide spectrum of characteristics. The core features are social difficulties, self-stimulatory behavior, areas of intense interest, and sensory difficulties. No two autistics are exactly the same, though. So, for me, I can mostly get by in daily life. I'm verbal—like, I can talk to people—and sensory problems aren't overwhelming for me, or I can usually deal with them. I struggle a lot with the social stuff, but in ways that are often...not obvious to people.

"The way I'd describe it is lacking a social *intuition*, or feeling like everyone was born having read a book on how to communicate with others while I never got the book. Like, there are all these weird unspoken *rules* about what you should say or not say in conversation, rules that I don't know or that don't make sense to me. I don't often get it when people are hinting at something—if you want me to do or say something, you have to specifically tell me. And people are always reading things into what I say that I didn't intend to imply. Like, I tend to be direct—most autistics are—but people usually assume directness means you're royally pissed-off even though it's just...my default way of communicating. So I always feel like I'm balancing on the edge of a knife when I'm talking to people, because I never know when I might end up accidentally saying the wrong thing in the wrong tone and making other people hate me forever. And living in that kind of constant fear is exhausting.

"And, I mean, I said I'm verbal, but I still struggle with talking, just not in ways most people can tell. It takes a lot of energy—spoons, in disability jargon—to translate thoughts into words, and even more spoons to voice my thoughts in ways that don't come naturally to me. Like taking care to make sure I'm not coming off as too direct—that costs extra spoons, so to speak. Not that I'm trying to say politeness sucks. What I mean is, I slip up a lot more if I'm tired or stressed and lacking in spoons to begin with, but it's not because I intended to offend or hurt people's feelings.

"Most portrayals of autistics, and most beliefs about autistics by allistic—non-autistic—people, assume that it's a black-and-white, all-or-nothing disability, when really it's more like a spectrum of functioning. I can read really basic facial expressions—like, if someone's smiling or frowning—but not anything subtler than that. I have trouble reading people's feelings based on facial expression or tone alone, but for people I know well, I can guess if they're feeling upset based on whether they're deviating from normal patterns of behavior. I'm not always right, of course, but I am sometimes. I can figure out sarcasm most of the time, but it's like I have to go through a circuit of logical reasoning in my head in order to be able to tell whether it's sarcasm, and I've failed spectacularly on occasion. I don't have auditory comprehension problems generally, but it shows up if I'm really distracted. It's not a hearing disorder—I can hear the words just fine—but my brain will struggle to process them into language. And it's super embarrassing and hard to talk about, because most people would just assume, 'Oh, so English is your second language?' when…it's not. Not at all. English is my first language and I can barely speak a few words of Cantonese."

He was rambling at this point, and he knew it, but he felt like he was reading off a disclaimer to Jordan. Like "Hey, these are all my quirks so please don't get mad at me if they show up." Also, he probably should've warned Jordan before he got started that delivering information in a long monologue was an autistic thing, too.

"Most movies and stuff show autistics as always blunt to the point of rudeness because they don't care about other people's feelings. But that's not true." Even thinking about it now made his face heat up with helpless anger again. "I *do* care about other people, but other people don't always understand that because I don't show it in the ways they expect me to. And I've had a lot of bad luck in my relationships before, to the point at which I gave up on dating altogether because it just hurt too fucking much, because these are things about myself I can't change, even if I wanted to..."

He was basically making an anti-pitch to Jordan, and he cringed, going back to studying his floor. *Reasons to date Noah Lau: Actually, don't, because I've given up on relationships already.*

He heard Jordan's footsteps approach him. Then, Jordan spoke, in his gentle, honey-soft voice.

"Thank you for sharing that with me. It's...a lot of information." He paused. "I did...get a sense, sometimes, that the way you talked was different from other people, though I couldn't quite put my finger on the difference. I...I thought you didn't want to talk to Amy because she was a vampire..."

Noah's face flushed. "No! That—that wasn't it. Sorry. I'm just awkward. Super awkward."

Jordan nodded. "I shouldn't have assumed...I had no idea. And I'm sorry that I'm so ignorant about autism, but

I do want to learn because it's important to you. I...I don't know what happened in your past relationships, but I think—I think you're an amazing person, Noah." His voice caught a little, stumbling over the words. "You didn't have to do all of this for me, especially since you hated vampires, but you did anyway. You're fun to talk to, and so, so considerate. So please, don't feel like I wouldn't—want a relationship with you because you're autistic. Because I do."

Noah blinked hard, a sudden lump aching in his throat. No one had said that to him before, outside of his family, and he didn't know what to do with those words.

"Well...you did save my life." Then he realized what he'd accidentally implied. "Uh—not that that's the only reason I was being nice to you! I mean, I like you, too! Um." He covered his face and groaned.

To his surprise, Jordan laughed, softly.

"It's okay," Jordan said as he stepped closer. He leaned in, brushing his lips against Noah's in a soft kiss.

Noah had been here before. His bruised, jaded heart was scared to gamble with his feelings again. But hope had taken root and sprouted inside him, and he let himself believe that, maybe this time, the risk would be worth it.

Chapter Fifteen

Noah drummed his fingers anxiously against the steering wheel. It felt like every traffic light he'd encountered had turned red as soon as he'd come up to it, and it was driving him out of his mind.

Please let Jordan be okay, he prayed as he drove out of the city and into the suburbs. Obviously, being a vampire, Jordan was difficult to kill, but he could still feel pain just like the next person. And, as Noah knew all too well, he wasn't completely invincible.

Rob had replied to Noah's text by saying that he'd left the office and was at his house in Wellesley. Noah pulled up in front of his house, went up to the front door, and rang the doorbell.

"Thanks for seeing me," Noah said when Rob answered. "Sorry to bother you at this late hour…"

"It's no bother at all. Please, come on in."

Rob led him inside the house, through the wooden hallways decorated with pictures of his family to his office. "Melissa's gone to visit the kids, so I'm the only one left to play host, I'm afraid. Would you like anything to drink?"

"No, thank you." Noah sat across from Rob, on the other side of the desk.

"Your text sounded urgent. What can I help you with, Noah?"

Noah took a deep breath. Carefully, he explained what he'd found: that there seemed to be a group of people within the VHA who were identifying vampires that hadn't necessarily been proved to be dangerous and then making up evidence to send hunters after those vampires.

"And that's obviously wrong and against what the VHA stands for," Noah went on. "But also..." He swallowed hard, gathering his courage. "I've been...seeing someone. He's...a vampire. And I think Casey O'Donnell found out somehow, and now he's missing, and I'm—I'm worried that he could be in danger. So...I need your help."

Rob had steepled his fingers together on his desk, as though he were deep in thought. Noah waited.

"Tell me more about this...vampire that you're dating," Rob said. "When did this happen? How did you meet him?"

Noah's impatience was reaching its boiling point. "No offense, Rob," he said curtly, "but can I save the explanation for later? Right now, I'm just worried about where he is and if he's okay."

"He's a vampire," Rob said with a wave of his hand. "He's probably fine."

"Yeah, but what if he's not?" Noah fought to keep his temper under control. "The rogue faction—including Casey O'Donnell and who knows who else—has been killing vampires without checking to see if they've even attacked a human first. Jordan hasn't attacked anyone; he gets all his blood from the pills."

"How can you be sure?" Rob asked, giving him a look.

Noah was about ready to tear his hair out. "Gee, I don't know, I only *live* with the guy?"

Rob's eyebrows lifted. "Even so, you can't keep track of where he is every minute of the day, can you?"

Fucking hell, this conversation was turning into a trainwreck from Noah's worst nightmares. Still, he had no choice but to power through it. "Jesus, Rob. You're suspicious of him because he's a vampire, fine. But he hasn't done anything wrong, and he could be in danger—"

"Right, he's a *vampire*," Rob interrupted. "I'm just curious, Noah; don't you ever feel unsafe around him? He could drain your blood while you're sleeping, and you'd never wake up."

Noah couldn't wrap his mind around Rob's continuous attempts to derail the conversation. "*Clearly* he's never done that!" he nearly shouted.

"But he *could*."

"And I could grab an aspen stick and stake him in the heart while *he's* sleeping. Seriously, Rob, what the hell? I'm trying to tell you that there's someone fucking things up in the VHA and going after any vampire they find, and it's like you don't even *care*—"

He stopped dead.

There was only one plausible reason for why Rob wouldn't care, aside from the possibility that he'd completely lost his mind, and that was if he knew already.

And if he knew already, that meant...

"You're in on it," said Noah slowly. "Aren't you?"

When Rob failed to immediately protest, the gears in Noah's head gradually shifted to panic mode.

"O'Donnell—was Casey working for *you*? Don't tell me *you* sent him to my apartment?" Noah said, torn between shock and dismay.

"He'd been surveilling some vampire protesters when he happened to see you at a park with them one afternoon, and he overheard one of the protesters addressing your companion as one of them. I thought you'd just unknowingly befriended a vampire...until, while he was trying to determine the vampire's identity, he met that same vampire when he visited your apartment."

Noah's mind swam. *Fuck, fuck, fuck.* He shouldn't have...what, been out in public with Jordan? Engaged those protesters? But it wasn't like he could possibly have predicted that Casey would be nearby... And was *that* the reason Casey kept asking him about his friends? Because he was fishing for information about Jordan?

"I have to say, Noah, I *am* curious as to how you ended up deciding to sleep with a vampire."

Rob's tone made Noah's skin crawl. "Where's Jordan?" he asked bluntly. "What have you done with him?"

Rob sighed.

"Do you know the history of the VHA?" he asked as pleasantly as though they were discussing the weather.

It wasn't often that Noah thought *Screw history*, but right now, he had more urgent things to worry about. "*Where's Jordan?*" he repeated.

"Originally," Rob went on as though Noah hadn't said anything, "VHA hunters didn't necessarily distinguish between which vampires they went after. However, since they typically only found out about vampires through a trail of dead bodies, the vampires they hunted happened to be confirmed killers. But all of that was back in the analog days, before computers and surveillance began to make it possible to discover vampires without relying on a physical blood trail.

"There was a major, very bitter debate within the VHA when it went public as to whether they should target all vampires or only specific ones. The ones who argued for limiting our targets only to vampires who had been confirmed to have killed humans won out. Things were volatile in the wake of vampires going public, and our upper brass wanted to be cautious. Talks of creating blood banks soon began, and some people were optimistic that with blood banks, vampires would no longer have to kill to survive, and the VHA might eventually disappear altogether."

At any other moment, Noah would've been interested in this conversation—after all, he'd been a history major in college. Right now, though, he was confused and pissed. "What does any of this have to do with—"

"The ones who argued for targeting *all* vampires, however, didn't believe this. Humans kill one another often enough for little reason; what was the reason for believing vampires to be any different?"

Noah's fists clenched in his lap. "So...you were part of that group?"

Rob regarded him steadily until Noah had to look away, the direct eye contact making him uncomfortable.

"It was the right choice. The policy the VHA *should've* adopted."

"So...what, you've been delegating Casey—and other people—to make up information to incriminate vampires without waiting for proof first?"

"Why, would you rather wait until lives are lost before we put a stop to the bloodsuckers?"

Noah shook his head. "We're not exterminators. We stand for justice. Killing every single vampire isn't *justice*."

Rob stood up behind his desk and began to pace back and forth. "Of all the people who've bought into the pro-vampire propaganda, I never expected you would've been one of them."

Noah blinked. "I haven't bought into anything—"

"Then how can you talk as though I'm doing the wrong thing? After everything you've seen? You used to work in Investigations," Rob threw out. "You've counted the bodies."

Noah gritted his teeth. "I know. Okay? I *know*. Of course I know. But...the world isn't so black and white. Not every vampire is a serial murderer—"

"Hashtag #NotAllVampires?" Rob said with more contempt in his voice than Noah had ever heard from him before. He sat back down and leaned across the desk. "There's no such thing as an innocent vampire, Noah. Their blood thirst makes them ticking time bombs to humans."

"Humans kill one another all the time. Does that mean humans are too dangerous to be around?" Noah spat.

Rob raised an eyebrow. "But that's the thing, Noah. Whether one human decides to kill another depends on a conscious choice they make. A vampire, however, cannot make that decision. You know the science."

He did. Neurologists had discovered that, when a vampire experienced blood thirst, certain parts of their brains shut down, making them unable to resist the urge to kill.

Rob went on, "The blood thirst will drive them to murder anyone near them—friends, family, or *lover*—and they are helpless to fight it."

"Things are different now," Noah snapped. "Vampires can take blood pills. They don't have to kill if they don't want to—and Jordan *hates* killing."

"Regret doesn't change his biology." Rob sat back and regarded him. "What would your parents say if they were alive, Noah?"

Noah froze, all the air leaving his lungs as though he'd just been socked in the gut. *Oh. That was a low blow.*

"They're—they're not here," he stammered out.

"Exactly. And why is that, huh?" Rob leaned forward. "Can you honestly, in clear conscience, sleep with the same kind of creature that *killed your parents*?"

Noah stared at him, eyes suddenly prickling. That was unfair. That was *monstrously* unfair. Jordan wasn't the vampire who had killed his parents.

But Jordan has *killed people, hasn't he?* an unwanted voice whispered in the back of his head. Sure, Julius had forced Jordan to do it, but that didn't change the fact that, under VHA policy, Jordan would've been a target for elimination. And deep down, Noah didn't like to think about that. Maybe he was a hypocrite with compromised values. Or maybe he didn't want to think that the vampire who killed his parents, instead of being a sadistic killer, might have been starved and out of control, like Jordan had been.

"What do you want me to do?" His voice came out scratchy, hoarse, barely above a whisper. "I didn't—I didn't plan for this to happen. It just did."

He stared down at his hands until Rob gave a sigh.

"Noah...listen. I know it hasn't been easy for you, having Asperger's. Not being able to make friends easily, having a hard time deciphering people's true intentions, being vulnerable to manipulation and people taking advantage of you..."

Noah blinked and abruptly sat up straight, feeling as though he'd just been slapped in the face. Heat flooded his cheeks. "You think—you think he took *advantage* of me?" he spluttered. "Or are you trying to say I can't be trusted to make decisions about my own love life?"

"I'm just saying that maybe you weren't able to think things through, because of your disability—"

"Oh my God, that is such *bullshit*."

Noah's hands were shaking. He felt betrayed. He'd always thought Rob was one of the ones who understood, who didn't condescend to him.

"Jesus fucking Christ, I'm autistic, but I'm also a legal fucking *adult* who understands consent and consequences *just fine. Don't* talk to me as though I have the mental age of a child because that is goddamned *insulting.* Sometimes I might make shitty choices, but I don't see allistic adults doing much better!"

Rob pressed his lips together. "Noah, you don't understand—"

"Don't understand *what*? That he's a *vampire*? That's pretty fucking hard to miss," Noah retorted.

"And he'll always be a danger to you."

"He'd never hurt me," Noah snapped.

Rob raised an eyebrow and tapped his phone. The door to the room opened, and two VHA hunters entered. Noah tried to grab for his own phone, but they yanked it away from him and grabbed Noah by the arms.

"What—get off me!" Noah's head snapped back around to Rob. "Rob, what the fuck is this?"

"I'm sorry, Noah, but you need to learn."

"Learn *what*? Rob? *Rob!*"

Noah fought ferociously against the two men who dragged him out of the room—he didn't like to be moved against his will, and *he didn't like to be fucking grabbed by strangers*—but they shoved something into the back of his jeans—*wait, what?*—before they dragged him down the stairs into the basement. Then, they shoved him through another door and slammed it shut behind him.

Rubbing his arms where they'd gripped him, Noah sat up, grunting as whatever they'd stuck behind him poked him in the back. He reached around, grabbing a hold of it, brought it in front of his face—and stared in confusion.

It was a wooden stake.

The fuck?

Baffled, he looked around. He was in what appeared to be a boiler room, and it took him a moment to realize there was someone else slumped against the other side of the room. Someone who looked a lot like...

"Jordan!"

Noah nearly cried in relief. But then he spied a large, dark red stain on Jordan's shirt. He rushed over, leaving the stake on the ground. "Oh my God, is that blood? Are you okay? Are you—"

"Ngh...don't." Jordan pressed himself more tightly against the corner, opening his eyes. "Stay back," he said, his voice weak.

Noah froze. Jordan's irises had gone completely red—the color of a starved vampire.

"Don't," Jordan repeated in a broken whimper. "You have to get away from me."

"But you're bleeding," said Noah helplessly.

"I'm...fine." Jordan exhaled with a ragged breath. "You have to get out, Noah. I...I don't want to hurt you."

Noah felt awful just leaving him there, and yet...he knew Jordan wasn't lying. He stood up and went to try the door.

It wouldn't open.

"The door's locked."

Jordan made a distressed sound. "Please," he whispered. "You have to get out of here. *Please.*"

Noah was suddenly aware of the stake he'd left on the floor as though it radiated an icy chill. Rob wanted him to kill Jordan—and he'd purposely injured Jordan to trigger his blood thirst, in order to give Noah no choice.

Noah sank to the floor. "No," he said hoarsely. "No. There has to be another way."

Jordan shifted restlessly against the far wall. Noah didn't want to know how much willpower it was taking him to stay still, or how much longer Jordan could resist.

"Jordan." His voice trembled in fear in spite of himself, and Noah tried to clear his throat. "Could you...is it possible for you to just take *some* blood, not...all of it?"

Jordan stared at him with wide eyes, his scarlet irises alien against his face. He shook his head slowly. "Noah, *no*. It's...too dangerous. I can't..." A shudder went through him. "I don't have that much control. Right now."

Noah couldn't believe he was seriously considering this—seriously considering offering up his blood to a vampire. Who might kill him. This was literally a scene out of his worst nightmares. His throat felt dry; his heart pounded in his chest as though it were trying to escape his ribcage. But he couldn't even *consider* picking up the stake he'd left on the ground, and given the choice of one-hundred-percent death if he waited for Jordan to lose his mind and drain him completely, or ninety-something-percent death if Jordan fed now...

Noah swallowed hard. He began to roll up his left sleeve with shaking hands.

"What are you doing?" Jordan screwed his eyes shut and, for some reason, clamped his hands over his ears. His entire body was trembling. "Noah, *stop*—"

"If you wait, you'll have even less control. Just do it now."

Jordan still hesitated, but he finally crawled over, his movements jerky, eyes fixed on anything but Noah. When he took Noah's wrist in his hands, his fangs had elongated, and Noah had to look away.

He'd expected it to hurt, but the pain was surprisingly minimal—not even as bad as getting a shot. Noah felt strangely hazy, his mind floating in an oddly pleasant calm.

The calm eventually turned into lightheadedness, though, and when Noah looked down, alarm pierced his comforting haze. His arm had paled to the shade of paper, and Jordan was still feeding.

"Jor—Jordan." His voice had gone weak. *Oh, fuck.* "Jordan, stop. Please."

He tried to tug his arm free, but the effort made the room swim around him before the ground went sideways and everything collapsed into darkness.

Wet.

Noah's eyes fluttered at the damp sensation on his face. He was resting in Jordan's lap, with Jordan's arms around him. It took him a long moment to realize Jordan was crying.

"I'm so sorry," Jordan whispered. "I'm so sorry."

Noah reached up to pat Jordan's arm. "Shh. 'S gonna be okay." His words slurred with exhaustion.

"It's my fault." Jordan choked back a sob. "They told me they had you, and they'd hurt you if I didn't come along. It was all a lie. I shouldn't have believed them..."

Noah supposed he couldn't blame Jordan for that. If Jordan had a weakness, it was that he always wanted to resolve conflicts peacefully.

Jordan sniffled. "You should hate me." His voice was broken.

I don't, Noah thought. Maybe it was odd that, instead of panicking, he felt peaceful. Maybe it was the blood loss and vampire saliva in his veins messing with his brain. But somehow, he was convinced that either everything was going to be okay, or if it wasn't, it was beyond his control at this point.

Jordan opened his mouth, but then it snapped shut as he glanced up. Noah registered the sound of the door opening a split second before Jordan vanished from his side.

A split second before two gunshots cracked through the air, and Jordan collapsed backward onto the ground.

"*No!*" Noah screamed.

Jordan had a hand pressed to his chest, his T-shirt stained almost completely red. He grimaced before bringing his hand to his mouth, trying to suck the blood from it.

Noah tried to push himself up, but his arms were too weak. A weight descended on him—one of Rob's lackeys from before? His vision swam for a moment as someone wrestled with Jordan. When it cleared, he saw Rob pinning Jordan's arms and chest to the ground, Jordan snapping at Rob like a crocodile until Rob pushed the muzzle of his handgun against Jordan's forehead.

"Look at this monster, this *thing* you tried to call your lover," Rob said, his voice dripping with scorn.

"Stop." Noah's voice was weak, thin. Memories streamed through his mind: him and Jordan laughing at some cheesy rom-com, cuddling in bed and talking late into the night. So far from the thirst-driven bloodsucker he was now. "Please, Rob."

"Even after he nearly drained you? You're more brainwashed than I thought," Rob said with what Noah thought was a mix of pity and disdain. His finger twitched on the trigger.

"No!" Noah tried to crawl toward them, but Rob's lackey had him pinned down, and he was too weak. His vision blurred with tears that spilled down his cheeks. "Don't hurt him," he begged. "Don't hurt him, *please.*"

"This is for your own good, Noah."

Noah wrenched one hand free and tried to reach for Jordan. So close. Too far.

"I love you," he whispered.

Jordan's eyes widened. A crash sounded, and then the bang of a gunshot.

Noah's heart seized up. It took him a second to process the fact that Rob had dropped his gun.

"Director Robert Bellamy, please put your hands over your head and don't make any sudden movements," Ariel Cross's voice came from the doorway.

What the hell? Noah thought, his mind struggling to make sense of what was happening. He tried to raise his head, even though it felt so heavy, and either Ariel had triplicated herself or two other VHA personnel flanked her. *How...?*

Rob glared at the doorway. "This *vampire* just tried to drain Noah's blood, and you're shooting at *me*? Have you lost your goddamned mind?"

"You're expecting me to believe that, after Noah left to find you, he just *happened* to lock himself in your basement with a starved vampire?"

Noah lost track of the conversation, his senses dissolving into fuzzy static, and then blackness. The last thing he was aware of was watching Jordan's eyes blink at him, his lips forming the shape of Noah's name.

Chapter Sixteen

When Noah awoke, it took him a moment to realize that he was in the VHA's infirmary, lying down with a blood transfusion hooked up to his arm.

"Hey. Welcome back."

Noah tried to blink the fuzziness from his vision. Ariel was sitting next to his bed, smiling at him.

"What..." He cleared his throat. "What happened?"

"You fainted. Losing almost two quarts of blood will do that. So, you missed the part where we managed to get Rob Bellamy to surrender peacefully. He's under house arrest right now, waiting for VHA Internal Affairs to get here and sort this mess out."

"How did you know that I was...?"

"I tried texting you. When you didn't respond, I got worried and stopped by the office first, and then Rob's house when the people at the office told me he'd gone home for the day. Here's your phone back, by the way." Ariel put it on the table by the bed.

Noah had the presence of mind to be relieved; replacing his phone wouldn't have been fun for his wallet.

He turned his head, but he didn't see Jordan in the infirmary.

"Where's Jordan?" he asked, trying not to panic.

"He's fine," Ariel assured him. "We managed to give him enough blood for his wounds to heal before he, uh, attacked anyone. I was actually hoping to talk to him, but he left in a hurry."

"Oh." Noah exhaled. "He...probably just wanted to go home or something."

Ariel inclined her head. "Probably."

He swallowed hard. "I...I'm sorry. You were right about not trusting Rob, and I didn't listen. I'm such an idiot."

There was a brief pause before Ariel said, "Don't be too hard on yourself, Noah. It's easy to believe the best of the people we've known for a while. As the outsider, it was easier for me to be cynical."

Noah glanced at her; she was smiling at him, so he tentatively smiled back. He doubted he could trust anyone ever again after this, though.

"Anyway, Internal Affairs should take things from here, so you have nothing to worry about."

"What's going to happen?" Noah couldn't help asking.

"Rob will be fired, of course. Same for Casey. There will be an inquiry into the branch to root out everyone who was involved...and a new branch director will have to be appointed, of course. It's not going to be pretty."

Sounded like a mess, all right. Noah couldn't help feeling sorry for Rob for a moment, knowing how dedicated he'd been to protecting humanity from vampires.

But he crossed the line. And he was going to kill Jordan.

"Are you sure he'll be fired?" he found himself asking. The whole thing had made him even more cynical than he already was. "You're sure there's no one higher up who also shares his views?"

Ariel chuckled a little. "You're learning fast. But take it from someone with friends at VHA Central—they *are* becoming more careful about handling criticism from HemRC. Unfortunately, this whole series of events will probably cause a media circus."

"Great," Noah groaned. *Just great.* He could practically see the headlines: *VHA Corruption: How Far Does It Go?*

The worst part was, in pursuing his own misguided vision of justice, Rob had cast a shadow over VHA Boston's entire record, opening the door for HemRC to question every single vampire they'd targeted. And Noah was going to have to deal with his own guilt, too, for the role he'd played in Rob's crusade, however unwittingly.

"Um," he went on, anxiety making him mumble, "about Jordan..." He hesitated, swallowing hard. "Is he...is anything going to happen to him?"

"Well...he didn't kill anyone," said Ariel slowly.

"Right, but..." Noah's hands clenched in the sheets. "That's all? I just...I don't..." The words died in his throat, strangled by the shame that burned through him at his situation. He was a hunter. He couldn't beg for the VHA to forget about Jordan and leave him alone, just because Jordan was his boyfriend.

Just because Noah loved him.

"I told IA exactly what I saw," said Ariel. "That Rob captured a vampire and shot him to provoke him into attacking you." Quietly, she added, "Don't worry about it, okay?"

He wasn't sure if he could let go of his worries so easily, especially since his secret relationship with Jordan wasn't completely a secret anymore. And if there was any chance that Rob or Casey had told other people at the VHA about Noah's relationship with Jordan...the last thing he needed was yet another reason for people at work to look at him strangely. Or worse.

But there was nothing he could do other than trust Ariel's assurances for now. "Okay. Thank you," he whispered.

Ariel only nodded. "Just get some rest, all right?"

Noah quickly became antsy, though, at having to stay in the infirmary for an entire day, with nothing else to do except surf the internet on his phone. Especially since Jordan wasn't around. He knew, of course, that Jordan could heal from almost any wound as long as he had blood, but the last time Noah had seen him, he'd been shot multiple times, so Noah would've felt better seeing him with his own eyes.

Hey, missed you in the infirmary. Are you ok? Noah texted him.

I'm fine, Jordan replied a few minutes later, and Noah relaxed.

When they finally let Noah go, he had to trek out to Wellesley again to collect his car from Rob's place; then, he drove home in a cloud of impatience and took the stairs two at a time up to his apartment.

"Jordan?" he called out after he'd unlocked his door.

No response.

Oh, no. A surge of déjà-vu almost knocked him over. But this couldn't be happening *again*—how many vampire-kidnappers could possibly live in Boston?

As Noah glanced around the apartment wildly for clues, he realized there was a sheet of paper on the kitchen table, with a note written in Jordan's handwriting.

Noah—

I'm sorry.

J.

Noah stared at the note, rereading it over and over again until the words made no sense to him. What the hell did this mean?

Where did Jordan go?

Why?

Normally, after a life-threateningly stressful event, Noah would've crashed on his couch for a couple of days, caught up on Netflix and his favorite MMO, and chillaxed by limiting his interactions with people to his family and grocery store cashiers.

Instead, he had to haul his ass to Lexington to beg not-quite-strangers, but-not-exactly-friends for information. That was not his definition of "chillaxing."

"I'm sorry to bother you." After asking several people before the VSV meeting already, he practically had his speech memorized. "Have you seen Jordan?"

He braced himself for another *Sorry, no*, but Laura the-vampire-who-looked-like-a-punk-rocker pursed her lips. "Yeah, he's at my place."

Noah's brain took an agonizingly long moment to transition from expected disappointment to understanding. "Wait...he is?"

"Yeah. And he won't tell me what happened, except to say it was his fault."

Typical Jordan. "Can I...I mean..." It had occurred to Noah that the reason Jordan left was because he didn't want to talk to him, but he was dying to know *why*. "I just want to talk to him," he finished desperately.

Laura eyed him. Then she half shrugged, half nodded.

"Come with me after the meeting."

Noah accompanied Laura on the T to Roxbury, where she led him up to a studio apartment. When she unlocked the door, Noah saw a chaotic living room strewn with clothes and knickknacks—and Jordan sitting on the couch, shutting off the TV, looking healed and fine.

Noah was torn between wanting to kiss Jordan and wanting to ask him *Dude, what the fuck?* But the expression on Jordan's face—the way he didn't look happy to see Noah—stopped him in his tracks.

"I got your note," Noah blurted out as he heard Laura move to a different part of the apartment, leaving them alone. "But I just don't—I don't understand."

Jordan looked away. "I nearly *killed* you, Noah."

"Yeah, but that was all Rob's fault! He—he set you up because he wanted to force me into killing you. It wasn't *you*, Jordan—"

"Noah, stop. Please."

Noah's mouth clamped shut.

"I can smell your blood." Jordan had closed his eyes. "Always, whenever you're near. And it smells like something I want to drink. I can't...turn it off."

"Jordan—"

"I can hear your pulse, coming from every major artery. Do you understand?" His voice was heavy.

Noah's hands had clenched into fists. "You think I don't know any of this? That I didn't think about it when we started dating? Of course I did! But I *trust* you, Jordan. I know you never wanted to hurt me."

"Maybe it's not about what I want," Jordan murmured to the floor. "Maybe it's about what I *am*. And I'm a vampire. I'll always be a danger to you."

"Jordan—Rob fucked with your head, okay?" Noah's voice rose, shaking. *"It wasn't your fault."*

Jordan shuddered. "It doesn't change what I did. It doesn't change the fact that I hurt you." His shoulders hunched. "Maybe...he was right. Vampires and humans can't be together. So maybe...maybe it's better this way."

Noah wanted to argue against that with a long, articulate rebuttal worthy of a lawyer in cross-examination. Instead, all he could stammer was, "You can't—you can't say that!"

"I'm sorry, Noah," Jordan said, his voice small. "I just...I can't. I'm not human enough."

Noah's heart plummeted, shattering into tiny pieces. *No*, he wanted to cry, *no, don't say that! Not after everything we've been through together. Please, take it back.*

"Please," Noah whispered.

Jordan still wouldn't look at him. "I'm sorry."

Noah was left to stumble out of Laura's apartment in a daze, picking up the broken pieces of his heart along the way, wondering if it would ever be possible to fit them back together again.

Chapter Seventeen

FOUR MONTHS EARLIER

Noah sat at a quiet corner table in Mango Red, his fingers skating over the smooth surface of a bead lanyard he'd brought. He hadn't meant to come early, but Elsie had texted to say she was running a few minutes late after he'd already arrived, and so he was left to stew in anxiety while waiting for her.

Finally, Elsie walked through the front door, a red slouch hat covering her hair. She brightened up when she saw him. "Hey. Sorry to keep you waiting."

He tried to smile back. "It's fine."

"Tea?"

"Mango, please."

She went to get their orders and came back with two cups. She handed Noah his bubble tea and a straw (red, as always) and sat opposite from him. "I'd ask you how you're doing, but I have a feeling you've got something specific on your mind."

She knew him too well. "Um...yeah."

"So?"

Noah wrapped his lanyard around his fingers and bit his lip. "I'm seeing someone again," he blurted out before he could lose his nerve.

A grin spread across Elsie's face. "Tell me everything. Who is it?"

"Jordan—"

"Ha! I knew it."

"Don't look so smug," Noah grumbled. He looked down, swallowing. "I...I need to tell you something about him."

"More like you need to tell me *everything* about him." Elsie folded her arms. "But, okay, what's this one thing you need to tell me?"

Even though he'd received Jordan's blessing to tell her, Noah didn't want to say it out loud, in such a public place. He typed out *He's a vampire* in his phone and handed it to Elsie to read.

Elsie scanned the screen. She handed the phone back to him. "For real?"

He nodded.

She sat back in her seat, her expression unreadable. Noah's anxiety escalated.

"Please don't hate me." The words escaped from him before he'd had a chance to think.

She glanced up. "Of course I don't hate you. Sorry, it's just...I'm trying to process."

Noah poked at the tapioca bubbles at the bottom of his cup with his straw. "Because of Mom and Dad?"

"Because I thought you saw vampires as monsters."

Noah looked out the window to the street. There were plenty of things he could've said: *Jordan isn't a monster*, or *I didn't consider vampires that only get blood from pills*, or *Maybe I was wrong, just a little bit.*

Instead, he said, "Aren't there people who consider me a monster, too?"

He heard Elsie inhale sharply. "That's not—"

"Not the same, I know." He wrapped his hands around his plastic cup. "Autism doesn't drive anyone to drink blood. But there are those who think people like me shouldn't be allowed to exist." People who pushed for genetic testing for autism with eugenic goals; people who would rather have their children die of preventable diseases than—even though the theory had been thoroughly debunked—possibly "develop" autism from vaccines. "People who think we lack some—some fundamental humanity—"

"Fuck them."

"I know they're wrong," he said to his tea. "But when people treat you as inhuman, and they ostracize you because of it, there's a part of you that can't help feeling like it's true. That you must be a monster, and that's why no one likes you."

Being autistic didn't make him a monster, but other people's treatment of him made him feel like one. Ableism was death by a thousand cuts, the constant, relentless erosion of his self-esteem and sense of self-worth. And the subtle things were the most hurtful of all—the unconscious biases, the daily rejections by other people for being *just not normal enough*.

Elsie didn't respond. When Noah raised his head, he saw that she was looking down at the table, her fists clenched.

A stab of anxiety went through him. "Did I say something wrong?"

Slowly, she shook her head. "No. I just...I hate that I've been powerless to stop you from feeling that way."

A lump rose in his throat. "It's not your fault," he protested. "You did everything you could. I'm lucky, in a lot of ways..."

"I couldn't stop Aunt Leah and Uncle Matthew from being assholes and saying hurtful bullshit about you."

After their parents died, they'd lived with Aunt Leah and Uncle Matthew for a year before moving in with Aunt Crystal. It had taken Noah years to learn that his aunt and uncle didn't like him because he was autistic, because Elsie had hidden the truth from him. He'd wondered why Elsie always seemed cold to them, but he hadn't learned why until he was sixteen and he overheard a conversation between them and Elsie one Thanksgiving that left him reeling. He'd been hurt that Elsie hadn't told him earlier, at first, but later on, he had to admit that she probably did the right thing. How would he have reacted as a nine-year-old if he'd realized he'd been rejected by his aunt and uncle for being autistic?

I'm the eldest. Mom and Dad would've wanted me to protect you. That was what Elsie had told him, once, when he had an anxiety attack over the idea that she might have resented him. *Besides, we only have each other.*

"You did what you could," Noah repeated. "Anyway, my point was, I...feel for Jordan in some ways. That's all."

Elsie sipped her tea for a long moment, as though she were thinking, before she said, "Does he make you happy?"

Noah swallowed hard. He nodded. "Yeah. He does."

"Good." Elsie smiled. "That's all that matters."

The knot of tension inside Noah's chest loosened. He let go of the breath he'd been holding and smiled back at her. "Thanks."

"But if he breaks your heart, I'm going to kill him."

"Good luck with that," he said dryly.

He didn't want to think about heartbreak, though. He didn't want to think about the possibility of yet another relationship ending, because he was afraid of the idea that, once again, it would somehow be his fault.

Chapter Eighteen

Noah groaned as consciousness floated to him, wondering why his head ached. Then his bleary gaze landed on the bottles of scotch on his coffee table and he remembered that, for some reason, he'd thought it was a good idea last night to try to drink himself unconscious.

He was on week two of his post-breakup hangover, and it fucking sucked.

He lay on the couch, one arm flung over his eyes. God...he'd been here before. Beating himself up after yet *another* failed relationship. Scrutinizing his actions, everything he'd done and said, for some clue of what he'd done wrong. Slipping down a negative spiral of emotions until he was brooding over every painful mistake in his life.

Remembering every time someone had implied that he'd never get to have what allistic people could have, because of who he was.

He knew, logically, that it wasn't his fault. Yet a lifetime of being seen as a social weirdo had turned him paranoid. A lifetime of losing friendships and not understanding why, of realizing people thought him an asshole when he really wasn't trying to be, of studying allistic behavior and yet still failing to blend in. He liked himself the way he was, but in moments of weakness, doubt still crept in. A dark voice in the back of his head kept whispering, *Maybe Jordan just didn't like you, like everyone else. Maybe he finally decided you were too weird for him. Maybe Aunt Leah and all the books and movies were right about you, and you'll always be friendless and alone.*

His doorbell rang. For a second, his heart leaped at the thought that maybe Jordan had changed his mind, and he half rose from the couch to answer it—before he remembered his sister had texted him that she would drop by in the morning. He sank back down, trying not to feel too disappointed.

Elsie let herself in with her duplicate of his keys, carrying a plastic bag in her hand. She surveyed his apartment—the empty bottles of alcohol standing on the coffee table, the dirty dishes that had been left in the sink for days, the trashcan overflowing with takeout boxes. A pang of shame went through him.

"I'll...clean up later," he said in a hoarse voice.

"Are you sure? I can help."

He shook his head. "No, it's...it's fine. I can do it later."

"Okay. If you're sure." Elsie sat on the couch. "I'm going to murder Rob."

"Murder's bad," Noah mumbled. He struggled upright to give her some room, so she wasn't sitting on his legs.

"He nearly killed you."

"He didn't want me to die. He just wanted me to kill Jordan." The words came easily enough, but saying them out loud made Noah feel like he was stabbing himself in the chest.

"It was reckless endangerment of your safety, so same difference." Elsie sighed, looking over him. "How long has it been since you washed your hair?"

He didn't answer.

"Well...think about it next time you shower, okay?"

He leaned against her, feeling bad that his unwashed hair was probably rubbing grease stains into her shirt. Just another thing he was fucking up, on top of everything else.

"Els?"

"Yeah?"

He swallowed. "D'you think...Mom and Dad...would've been upset about me and Jordan?"

Elsie was quiet for a while before she sighed again. "Oh, Noah, I don't know. Maybe. Maybe not. Maybe they would've been more hung up about the fact that he was a guy. The thing is, they're gone, and it's impossible to know for sure what they would've thought."

He thought about that, but for once, the cold logic didn't soothe him.

"This is why I didn't want to do another relationship," he mumbled into Elsie's shoulder. "It's the breakups that kill me."

Elsie wrapped an arm around him. "It happens to the best of us. And yeah, it sucks, but you'll survive."

Noah made a skeptical noise. He wasn't so sure about that.

Elsie gave him a comforting squeeze and reached over to grab the plastic bag at her feet. "I got you some rice noodle rolls and red bean soup. Are you hungry?"

He shook his head.

"I'll leave them in the fridge, then." She eyed him. "And you probably need something non-alcoholic to drink. And then we can bust out the video games."

She boiled some chrysanthemum tea for them, and they spent the next few hours beating up computer-controlled opponents in Mario Kart and Super Smash Bros. Noah's spirits lifted, but when Elsie had to bow out for a prior engagement (because, unlike him, she actually had a social life), he was left once again lying on the couch, staring up at his ceiling.

Ariel had put him on leave—two weeks, minimum. He wondered if it was a sort of apology for what he and Jordan had gone through thanks to Rob. Or maybe it was incentive not to sue for assault and battery by his workplace supervisor. On one hand, he didn't have the energy to do anything, but on the other hand, it might've been nice to have some tedious paperwork to fill out just as a distraction.

Sighing, he finally dragged himself off the couch to boil some more water for tea. He didn't have the energy for it now, but he thought maybe he should try to reconnect with people on the autism forum he used to browse before he'd had a mental breakdown at the end of college and he'd gotten anxious even about online chatting.

Hey, it's not like you need a relationship to survive. Look at Aunt Crystal.

The difference between him and his aunt, though, was that she didn't want a romantic relationship, while he *did*. As cheesy, clichéd, and downright unrealistic as it was, he'd always dreamed of the fairytale romance. He wanted someone he could come home to, someone he could lean on and who could lean on him in turn, someone he could share everything in his life with. And he was too much of a failure at keeping friends—even more of a failure than other autistics—to substitute friendship for romance. For a few brief, shining months, he thought he'd finally had what he'd always wanted...only for it to crumble into dust. Again.

He closed his eyes and massaged the bridge of his nose. *Shut up, brain. Think happy thoughts. Or at least think about something else.*

There was nothing really to do except bury this pain, the way he'd buried so many others in a graveyard deep within his heart. He popped in his earbuds and played, on repeat, his most recent favorite song while he sat on the couch with his blanket around his shoulders and sipped his chrysanthemum tea. He had the rest of the week to hang out without having to interact with people; he might as well enjoy it as much as he could.

The doorbell rang again, and at first he thought Elsie had forgotten something at his place, but then it rang a second time a minute later. Frowning, Noah pulled his earbuds out, set his mug down, and made his way to the door. He hadn't ordered any groceries or takeout, but once in a while he got a wrong delivery—someone kept forgetting to clarify to pizza delivery guys that they lived in unit *fifteen*, not *fifty*.

He opened the door, expecting to fix Wrong Delivery Person with a hungover scowl—until he saw who was at his doorstep.

"J-*Jordan*?" he stammered.

Dressed in a plaid button-up shirt and jeans, Jordan looked as fresh as a model who'd just stepped out of a photo shoot. Meanwhile, Noah knew his bedhead and rumpled, days-old pajamas practically screamed "This Loser Can't Get Over a Breakup."

"Hi," said Jordan softly. "Can I come in?"

Mutely, Noah opened the door for him. Jordan settled down on the couch and, not knowing where else to sit, Noah sat at the opposite end from him, the space between them feeling like a No Man's Land.

They sat in heavy, awkward silence. Jordan's gaze drifted around the apartment, and Noah winced, remembering what a mess it was. He wished he'd cleaned it up beforehand, even though he knew he was totally lacking in the executive function to do so; all he'd been able to do was stare at the dirty dishes in his sink, his mind blanking out instead of grasping the steps he needed to wash them.

His mind raced with things he wanted to say, and yet he bit down on his tongue, afraid of saying the wrong thing and messing everything up again. But as the silence dragged on, the words bottled up inside Noah's throat until he felt like he was a volcano about to erupt, and he couldn't stay silent, waiting, any longer.

"Jordan," he began in a shaky voice, "I don't know if you came here to break up with me for good or whatever, but—don't. Please, don't. I know what happened was fucked up, and it fucked everything up. Somehow, we keep finding ourselves in shitty situations, and it fucking sucks. But I don't want what happened to be the reason for us to be over. I don't. Please."

It was one of the least eloquent speeches he'd made in his life, and he was a blubbering mess by the end. Jordan was staring at his hands clasped in front of him.

"I've been...thinking about what you said," Jordan began.

Noah wiped the back of his hand across his face and blinked. His heart beat a little faster, hoping against hope.

Jordan exhaled, slowly. "I'm...sorry. I know...I shouldn't have run off like that. I just...I felt so awful about what I did. I was scared to face you again," he finished in a whisper.

Noah swallowed hard. "You didn't have to be scared. Of me."

"I hated the fact that you...that you had to see me like that," Jordan said, his voice cracking.

Noah couldn't say that he hadn't been scared, because...well, he had been. It had been fucking terrifying. "It wasn't your fault" was all he could say, even though the words had done nothing to convince Jordan to stay the first time.

Jordan dropped his gaze. "I...I don't know. There was always a voice in the back of my head, telling me that I wasn't good enough for you. And when this happened, it just...felt like that voice had been right all along."

Noah's hands tightened into fists. "Well—well that voice is a lying asshole, okay? Just because Julius made you feel like shit for not being exactly what he wanted you to be, doesn't mean that he was right. He was *wrong*." He let his hands relax and forced himself to take a deep breath. "I know—I know it's not always easy to get rid of the fears that have been ingrained in us. For a long time, I thought I was unlovable because that was how I saw autistic characters in books and movies being portrayed. I got knocked down in my relationships, a *lot*. Oftentimes it wasn't even really my fault, but I still blamed myself. I thought, maybe everything people always said about autistics not being able to have relationships was true. But then I met you."

Noah exhaled sharply. The words hadn't been easy to say, but he needed to say them.

"And yeah, I really didn't expect to fall in love with you. But..." He was getting choked up over his words, but he forced himself to go on, "but you accepted me for who I was, and you made me happy. And that kind of happiness, to me, is worth fighting to hold on to."

That was it. He'd given it his all, and now he was trembling, drained by his emotions, having used up all the words he'd had. He wished he had the ability to be more eloquent; raw honesty was all he could offer instead.

He heard Jordan get up, his footsteps approaching. Just as Noah worked up the courage to raise his head, he felt Jordan's hands against his face, Jordan's lips against his.

"Noah," he murmured. "Noah, I'm sorry. I don't want us to be over, either."

All of Noah's anxieties and frustration and grief had coalesced into a tightly wound ball that now cracked with relief, overwhelming him. He sobbed into Jordan's shirt.

Jordan cradled his face, fingers brushing against his disgusting hair. "I'm sorry," he said, over and over again. "I'm sorry for hurting you. I was such a mess after what happened that I just...broke. It wasn't you, Noah. It was never you."

Noah snuffled. He got that; he did. He knew better than anyone that people didn't always react gracefully when shitty things happened. "Just...if there is a next time, can we please just face it together?"

"Okay," Jordan whispered.

He stood up from the couch, and Noah latched on to his shirt in a panic before he realized Jordan was sitting down next to him. Noah ended up flopping over, his head resting on Jordan's thigh. He lay there for a moment, reassuring himself that Jordan was solid and real, before he rolled over to look up at Jordan's face.

"What changed your mind?" Noah murmured.

Jordan was quiet for a minute. "I don't know if anything changed my mind so much as time and space convinced me not to be a coward." He gave him a wobbly smile. "And…to be honest, Laura kicked me out. She said I was nuts to ignore such an 'obviously devoted guy'."

Noah mustered the energy to smile back. "Well, you were. No offense."

Jordan chuckled a little. His fingers moved through Noah's hair, and Noah cringed.

"Uh…you probably shouldn't. I haven't washed my hair in…um…long enough that you shouldn't be touching it."

Jordan's fingers drifted away. "Do you need help?"

Noah sucked in a breath. Executive dysfunction was one of the things he hated asking for help for because he felt embarrassed and because he'd gotten negative reactions before. It was not something most allistic people could understand. *"You can get an A in calculus, but you can't even take care of personal hygiene?"* one college ex-girlfriend had asked incredulously. Even though Jordan's voice was gentle, Noah could still barely bring himself to answer.

"I…I can take care of it," he said weakly. "I don't want to be a bother."

Jordan snorted softly. "Do you really think asking me to get in the shower with you is a 'bother'?"

"Okay, when you put it *that* way…"

"Just…if you want," said Jordan gently. "You don't have to, of course. But you're always telling me it's okay to ask for help, and I want you to know it's okay for you, too."

Damn it. Because, of course, Noah was much better at giving advice than following it himself, when he had his own internalized ableism to unpack still. But there was no way he could say no to Jordan after that.

"Fine," he said, feeling a strange mix of grudgingness and relief.

He let Jordan lead him to the bathroom, into the shower stall. He shucked off his clothes and turned the water on—that much he could do, at least—before he heard Jordan get in behind him, his shampoo-slick hands running through Noah's hair.

Noah closed his eyes, sighing as Jordan's soapy fingers moved gently over his scalp, breathing in the scent of citrus. It wasn't sexual, but it didn't need to be. He just stood there, soaking in the closeness, the feeling of being cared for and accepted, which filled his heart until he thought it would overflow with happiness.

This, he thought, was as close to paradise as he'd ever get.

Chapter Nineteen

As a vampire hunter, Noah was used to being in weird places at odd times. Visiting the cemetery with his boyfriend, however, was a whole other level of eccentric.

It took Noah a moment to realize that Jordan was hanging back by the entrance.

"Are you sure this is a good idea?" he asked when Noah turned to look at him.

Noah rolled his eyes. "I don't get why you're so anxious. It's not like my parents can disapprove of you from beyond the grave."

Jordan frowned at him. "I just...I don't know if I should be here," he mumbled.

Noah's heart sank a little. Jordan had agreed when Noah initially told him his idea, but then again, he'd come to realize that Jordan sometimes had problems saying "no." He stepped back over to him.

"We don't have to be here if you don't want to be," he said. "I know it's not exactly, you know, a romantic way to spend the day..."

Jordan glanced away, swallowing. "It just...feels kind of blasphemous for me to be here," he muttered.

"Blasphemous?" Noah echoed. "Well, my parents weren't religious..."

"That's not it." Jordan made a gesture that Noah had no idea how to interpret before he said, "You don't feel weird? At all? About me being here? Because of...of how your parents died?"

That was the same excuse Noah had given to Elsie a week ago. Noah stepped closer, lowering his voice. "*You* weren't the one who killed them."

"Yeah, but..." Jordan's voice trailed off.

When he was pretty sure Jordan wasn't going to finish his sentence, Noah said, "My parents are important to me, and you're important to me, too. So I'd like to introduce you to them...if that's okay."

After a long pause, Jordan finally let out a breath and nodded. The sky was clear that morning, the air crisp and cool. The fiery-colored leaves had begun peeling off the surrounding trees, crunching underfoot as they made their way through the cemetery, stopping in front of Noah's parents' tombstones.

The cemetery was quiet, and for a long moment, Noah was afraid to break the silence. At last, he cleared his throat.

"Hi, Mom. Hi, Dad. Uh...this is Jordan." He gestured beside him. "He's...the person that I'm dating. He's really amazing and kind and, um...yeah."

What had seemed to be an articulate, defiant speech in his head dissolved into barely coherent mumbling. Noah stood there for a moment, trying to gather the words to salvage his monologue, but he couldn't. He gave up, swallowing, and turned to Jordan instead.

"I...um..."

He stumbled over the words he wanted to say, turning them into gibberish. Jordan just waited patiently, watching him. Cheeks warm, Noah shook his head at himself.

"I want to say that my parents would've loved to meet you," he blurted out. "But the truth is, I have no idea. I didn't know them well enough since, you know, they died when I was a kid..."

Oh my God, stop talking. You are the least romantic person ever, a voice berated him in the back of his head. He bit the inside of his cheek before rushing on.

"But, no matter what, I don't regret meeting you," he said, adding in a mumble, "Just...in case you didn't know..."

He was beginning to think his whole idea was just stupid when a brush of warm, dry lips against his cheek stunned him. Jordan normally avoided PDA like the plague. Or, well, like someone who'd grown up terrified of being outed from the closet.

"Thank you," Jordan whispered, his eyes bright.

Noah looked away. "Stop that," he muttered. "You're going to make me cry, and I *hate* crying in public."

Jordan laughed a little huskily. "There's no one else around. Besides, we're in a cemetery. I'm sure no one would mind."

"Five out of five stars for most romantic spot to take your date mate?" Noah deadpanned. "That's what comes from dating a weirdo."

"I like your weird." Jordan was smiling, though his tone sounded serious. "Without a doubt, you're the most amazing person I've ever met."

Aww. Noah's face felt hot again, but for a different reason this time. "Okay, flatterer. I say it's time to go home."

"Sounds good to me."

They left the cemetery and set off together. Noah found himself stepping with his toes, bouncing with a kind of energy that filled him up and made him feel as though he could walk straight up into the sky.

And for once, he didn't care what everyone else passing him by on the street might think. Because the person who mattered most was smiling at him.

Acknowledgements

Thank you to NineStar Press for giving a home to this story about a queer and autistic character of color, and thanks especially to Raevyn McCann for the editorial guidance and Natasha Snow for the amazing cover.

And thank you, as always, to Stephanie and Rachel for cheering me on.

About the Author

E.S. Yu is the author of EIDOLON, a queer science fiction featuring assassins, tech conspiracies, and mental health discussions. E.S. is a lifelong lover of speculative fiction, video games, and superheroes. The stories E.S. writes often reflect darkness and injustice, from the perspective of a multiply marginalized person, while always believing in the power of healing and hope for a happy ending. An immigration attorney in a past life, when not writing, E.S. can be found drinking a lot of green tea and, of course, thinking about her next novel.

Email: esyuauthor@gmail.com

Facebook: www.facebook.com/aetherquill

Twitter: @aetherquill

Website: www.esyuwrites.wordpress.com

Other books by this author

Eidolon

Also Available from NineStar Press

Connect with NineStar Press

www.ninestarpress.com

www.facebook.com/ninestarpress

www.facebook.com/groups/NineStarNiche

www.twitter.com/ninestarpress

www.tumblr.com/blog/ninestarpress